Code Blue

HESHAM A. HASSABALLA

Faithful Word Press
Hinsdale, IL

ISBN: 0985326506
ISBN-13: 978-0985326500

DEDICATION

*In the Name of my Precious Beloved, to Whom all praise is
due forever and ever.*

Also, to my darling wife, without whom I am forever lost.

CONTENTS

ACKNOWLEDGMENTS

I send my deepest thanks to Mr. Alex Kronemer and Mr. Michael Wolfe at Unity Productions Foundation. Their support of me and my passion for writing has inspired me more than they can ever know. To them, I will be forever grateful.

1

The fog was still thick and heavy over the ground. The headlights of the sleek and shiny silver Bentley sedan could barely be seen as the thin two-lane road made them snake through the dense forest. The dew was dripping off of the tall, thick grass at the base of the forest, and the orange sunlight was just peeking over the horizon, making the thick fog shine more brightly white than before. The driver could barely be heard breathing as he drove, listening to the morning news on the radio. He was a distinguished, tall, and thin man. The few remaining black hairs on his head have joined the rest in a brilliant gray, with some white flecks in the mix. His face is also tall, with an almost square chin, high thin cheeks and broad forehead. Anyone who saw Dr. L. William Bryant knew he was a man of importance, even without knowing who he actually was.

Dr. Bryant was head of Cardiovascular Surgery at Chicago Memorial Hospital, and he was also just named the Alfred J. Harrison Chair of Surgery. The ceremony and party in his honor was today. His career could not have been more distinguished (though he did burn quite a few bridges to reach such a distinguished stature). As far as he was concerned, however, that did not matter because everyone had to come to him for everything. *It's good to be the chief,* he would always say to both himself and his often resentful and jealous colleagues. To make this day even more special, it was his 25th wedding anniversary. That's why he made sure he drove to the cemetery where his father was buried.

The entrance was ahead to the right, and as he turned into Rose Cemetery, the sun began to shine brightly across the wet, gray earth. The previously dense, thick fog was quickly burning off. It was a crisp, May morning, a bit chillier than normal, but that was nothing new for Chicago. His father was buried in section 33, and Dr. Bryant could practically drive to the gravesite in his sleep. Always calm and reserved, and a bit cold most of the time, he began to quiver a little as he got out of his car and walked up to his father's grave. Dr. Bryant normally visits his father's grave every year on his own birthday. But, that was a few months away, and this day was such a special day; he just could not wait.

He walked up to the grave: a modest site, with a small rectangular slab of marble that read: "L. William Bryant. Born 1934. Died 2004." His Italian leather

2

shoes were already soaked with the dew from the grass. As he stood over the slab, he said in a low voice, "Today, I am being named the Alfred J. Harrison Chair of Surgery. It's also my and Annie's 25th anniversary."

There was a deep-seated bitterness in his voice. And as he finished a memory bombarded his mind. He tried to suppress it, but he simply could not resist. The screams were muffled as the young woman pleaded with her drunk (and violent) husband: "Please, please, I didn't mean it. Please, please!"

The crash of a vase full of the freshly cut roses given to her the day before startled the young boy listening to this desperate exchange down the hall. He couldn't take his mother's crying anymore and dashed to his parents' bedroom in a fit of rage, bursting the door open.

He then beheld his mother, face bloodied and top ripped off, on the floor crying; his father was standing over her in a fit of rage, fist raised in the air. When his father realized what had happened, he lunged at the boy, only 10 at the time, and punched him in the face. He fell crying on the floor, and his father then picked up the boy and threw him out of the bedroom screaming, "You get the fuck out of my bedroom!" The door slammed, and his mother's screams commenced.

At this, Dr. Bryant regained his composure, tears streaming down his face. Angered by the fact that he let this memory get to him, he wiped the tears from his face and clenched his fists. He quickly turned around to leave when he abruptly stopped and came back to the grave. He spit on the marble slab, turned back to his car, and drove off. He came every year, in fact, to his father's grave to spit on it, this despite its being 50 miles away from his home. Moreover, although his name should have been "L. William Bryant, Jr.," he officially took off the "Jr." from his name, in order to make his disdain for his father even more evident.

He regained his composure before he left the cemetery, and all the refinement and sophistication that was temporarily dislodged by the memory of his father's abuse returned in full force. He was on his way to the hospital when he received a page. He looked at the pager and then yelled out to his voice activated telephone: "Dial CCU."

The phone rang once and a voice filled the interior of his car:

"CCU, this is Marge, how can I help you?"

"This is Dr. Bryant," in a most annoyed voice.

"One moment, Dr. Bryant," replied the unit secretary, "Annie paged you."

As the hold music - Mozart's Piano Concerto No. 24 - played, his frustration and impatience grew exponentially. His face also grew redder with each passing moment.

"Dr. Bryant?" said the young voice, interrupting Mozart.

"Why are you paging me?" Dr. Bryant screamed. "What is so important for you to bother me?"

"I am sorry Dr. Bryant..."

"That is what the fellows and residents are for!" yelped Dr. Bryant, interrupting Annie, now near tears.

"CALL THE FELLOW!" he screamed. Each time he spoke to her, his voice became louder and louder. He then hung up his voice-activated phone system.

He was breathing heavily and his face was as red as the sun when it first rose that morning. Yet, again, he quickly regained his composure and drove the rest of the way to the hospital without incident...or page.

2

"NO!"

She woke up with a start. She was sweating profusely, her curly brown hair soaked. Her brown eyes were already wet with tears, and they were streaming down her round, white face. Her scream awakened her husband who noticed she was crying and reached over and hugged her head, calmly soothing her crying.

"Another bad dream, baby?" he asked, turning on the bedroom light.

She nods, sniffling and wiping the profuse tears from her face. "I just can't get those dreams out of my head. I thought they were gone, but once I decided to go back, they all came back...and do not want to let up." She cried more intensely.

"Are you sure you want to do this?" he asked her, his voice full of concern. "You don't have to go back. We have a great life here together. You haven't been this happy in years. Your smile has never been more full. Why ruin all that?"

"I have to do this!" she snapped. "I can't fully heal if I don't! I will never be able to move on. We've been through this before!"

Her sudden rage and anger, which temporarily dried her tears, took her husband of two months, Jonathan Meyers, visibly aback.

"I'm so sorry, honey," she said, as she started to sob in Jonathan's arms. "I am so sorry."

"Hey, hey, it's okay, it's okay, baby," he said. "It's okay, my love."

He tried, as best he could, to console his clearly inconsolable new wife. They had first met three years ago. He was a social worker at the women's shelter in which Sarah was staying. She had run away from her home when she was 15 years old. She was homeless for a few years, and then she moved from shelter to shelter until she finally settled in the women's shelter in Seattle, where Jonathan had worked for the previous five years. As soon as he saw her, there was something about her that intrigued him. He felt almost compelled to help her, and he really could not understand why.

His initial attempts to help her were immediately rebuffed and rejected. Every man in her life - prior to that time - has meted out unspeakable treatment to her. Yet, he persisted in his attempts to gain her trust, and again, he really had no idea why. At first, tremendous pity moved him to help her learn to trust again.

With time, however, his feelings changed. He never intended to fall in love with her; he did not want to fall in love with her. But, he couldn't help it. There was something about her that he loved so dearly: it was not her physical looks, although she was quite an attractive young woman. It was more than that; there was something deep down in her soul that he loved immensely. It was as if their spirits were yearning to meet each other, and when they did, they were inseparable.

"Is it the same dream, honey? Is your father beating you?" Jonathan asked.

It took Sarah a very long time to answer.

"Sarah?" Jonathan asked, now a bit worried. "What's the matter?"

She started to cry once again.

"He was on top of me, thrusting into me. He had his hand over my mouth, so that my mother and brother would not hear my screams. When he would do that, I could not breathe, and it made it all the more horrifying. I would normally close my eyes and fly away to some place far, somewhere he can't hurt me. Before long, he would have his fill and leave me. But this time, and I don't really know why, I opened my eyes and saw my mother looking at us. She just walked away and did nothing. I started to scream, but he only pushed his hand more forcefully over my mouth. When even that didn't manage to stop me from screaming, he slapped me."

Her crying continued, "It must have been loud - his slap across my face. The next thing I knew, my brother barged into my room and pushed my father off of me. My father punched him in the stomach and threw him out of the room..."

Her sobbing became uncontrollable now.

"...and then...then...he came back and finished with me."

"You never told me that your father raped you. You...you...never..." Jonathan began to cry himself, his hands over his mouth in horror and then anger.

"I was ashamed...I thought you would not want me once you knew."

Jonathan's face pained when he heard this, tears streaming down his face. He reached out and held her face: "How could I be ashamed of you?"

Sarah hugged Jonathan and then released him.

"This went on for years. I even got pregnant, and he

made me get an abortion. It was then when I ran away from home," Her sobbing waned a bit.

"But do you know what was most hurtful?" Sarah interjected. "My mother *knew* what was happening but did nothing...nothing! How could she? How could she?" Sarah's tears continued to flow unabated.

Jonathan held his wife in his arms and gently rocked her the rest of the night. Sarah finally calmed down and fell asleep. Her crying exhausted her.

Thankfully, he woke up close to the time she had to go to the airport. He woke her up gently and said,

"Baby, it's time."

Wiping the sleep from her eyes, she got up and went into the bathroom to take a shower and freshen up. Jonathan went to shower in the hall bathroom, and he came back when she was already dressed.

"Are you *sure* you want to do this, babe?" Jon asked. His eyes full of concern.

"We're not going through this again..."

"OK, OK. I'm just worried about you." He pulled her towards him and held her in his still wet arms. "You have been on edge ever since you decided to go back and face your parents."

"*You're* the one who taught me to stop running from my past!" she snapped back at him.

"I know, but I didn't think you would actually *take* my advice," Jonathan said smiling.

"I married you, didn't I?" she smiled back.

"I'm so glad you did, my love." He embraced her and gave her a passionate kiss. He wanted to do more, but Sarah stopped him.

"Um, no. Baby, we need to get to the airport...and your all wet."

"Damn!" Jonathan said disappointed.

"You thought we had time for that? Is that all I am to you? A receptacle for your passions?"

"You *know* that is not true, honey!" Jonathan said. He always resented that comment from his wife.

"Just teasing you, Mr. Meyers," Sarah said playfully.

She reached over and kissed him to ensure to him that she was only joking.

"No time for a quickie?" Jonathan said pleadingly. Sarah rolled her eyes.

"NO! Now get dressed and meet me downstairs," Sarah said sternly.

She handed him his clothes; he was only in a towel.

"I'm going to go start the car, Jon," Sarah said, already heading toward the stairs. Sarah packed her bags days before and already put them in the trunk of their Toyota Camry.

"You're not having any breakfast, babe?"

"I'm not hungry," Sarah said, shouting from the kitchen.

Jonathan hurried downstairs to catch his wife.

"Yeah, but I am, babe. Can't I at least have a cup of coffee?" Jonathan asked, almost begging.

"We'll stop off on the way! What a baby! Maybe that's why you're scared of having kids," Sarah said smiling.

"Kids?"

Sarah laughed out loud. They both headed out to their car. The day was cool, but sunny, a rarity in the Pacific Northwest. The Sun was already high in the sky, and the trees were whistling in the brisk wind. They lived in a densely wooded subdivision of duplex townhomes, with neatly manicured green lawns and two-car garages. The mailboxes were all embedded in an all brick mini-tower, with the house number etched in stone. The neighborhood was quiet, everyone was away at work and school. They pulled out of their garage and wound along the smoothly paved suburban street and out of their subdivision.

They stopped along the way at one of the dozens of

local Starbucks to get a cup of coffee for Jonathan - Venti Mint Mocha with extra whip cream. Sarah still didn't want anything to eat.

"You have to eat something, Sarah," Jonathan said, sipping his very large cup.

"I'll get something at the airport...when I feel like it," Sarah said, a little annoyed at his persistence. She was in no mood for eating at this point.

As they turned toward the expressway, Sarah's mood visibly became darker. The sign above their heads read, "Airport exit." Jonathan noticed her change in facial expression and tried to make some small talk...quite unsuccessfully. Sarah didn't answer him and just continued to look out at the ocean in the distance.

"OK, I'll shut up now," Jonathan said, sipping his coffee and driving at the same time.

"I just don't want to talk, OK?

"You were fine just a few moments ago..."

"Jonathan..." Sarah whined.

"OK, OK, I'll shut up now," Jonathan repeated. The silence was deafening in the car the rest of the way to the airport terminal. He stopped the car at the American Airlines gate and popped open the trunk to get her bags for her.

Sarah was very slow to get out of the car. In fact, she sat inside the car, with the door open, facing the doors of the airport terminal, motionless as Jonathan walked up with her bags.

"Hey, are you OK?" Jonathan asked worriedly. He hated seeing how stressed Sarah look and not being able to help.

Sarah came out of her daze.

"Yeah, yeah. I'm fine," Sarah said. Sarah got out of the car and took her bags from her husband. She looked at him with eyes full of deep love and deep gratitude.

"Take as long as you need. You need to do this right. Don't worry about me. My girlfriend already misses me," Jonathan said smiling.

Sarah looked at him angrily but could not help but laugh. He could always make her laugh, even when she had no reason or desire to do so. It was one of the many things that made her fall in love with him in the first place.

"I'll call you when I get there," Sarah said, and she kissed Jonathan, who kissed her back passionately.

"Have a safe trip, baby. I miss you already," Jonathan said.

"Bye," said Sarah walking toward the automatic airport terminal door. She watched as Jonathan got back into the car and drove away, merging smoothly into the flowing traffic. When he was out of sight, she turned, took a deep breath, and entered the terminal. She looked left and right for the American Airlines desk, and she finally found the desk labeled "Domestic Departures."

She walked to the back of the line and waited until it was her turn. As she pulled out her driver's license and ticket, she looked around at the throngs of people walking to and fro, going to their respective destinations across the country and around the world.

Her thoughts then turned to what she was about to do, and her heart began to race and sweat was beading on her forehead. *What is it going to be like? What would she say? Would they even recognize her? How is Bobby doing? What would he say?* She went into another daze when she was brought out by a loud "Next, please!"

"I'm sorry," Sarah said as she rushed to get to the ticket counter.

"Ticket and identification, please," said the ticket counter employee. Sarah handed over both her license and E-ticket.

"Where are you flying, today?" asked the employee. Her name was also Sarah.

"Chicago..."

3

It can be seductive. The piercing quiet is only mildly disturbed with the rhythmic beeping of the oxygen monitor, the rhythmic beeping serenading you as you delve into another world, the world of the human body, cut open for the surgeon to manipulate and alter. The room, although cold and callous, is also clean and neat. All the surgical instruments are lined up neatly for the surgeon to use on a table sitting immediately next to the operating table, on which the patient lies. The walls are lined with pale, blue bricks, and the floor is as black as a moonless night. Although the room is already brightly lit, the operating table beams with the baseball-stadium-bright operating room lights, whose handles are sterile to not make the surgeon's hands dirty.

The operating table is in the middle of the room, underneath those lights, with a "scrub nurse" standing over all those neatly-lined instruments. Along the walls are a number of cabinets which contained a number of surgical gloves, supplies, and other tools that may be needed during a routine operation.

Surrounding the operating table is the surgeon and his assistants, three to be exact: a senior fellow, a senior resident, and a medical student holding the clamps to keep the operating area open for the surgeon. Everyone, including the scrub nurse, is dressed in full surgical gear: hair covering, face mask, blue sterile surgical gown, sterile gloves, and shoe coverings. There is another nurse, the circulating nurse, who is not dressed up in full surgical gear, who walks around the room getting supplies for the surgical team, which cannot touch anything outside of the immediate operating area. She does, however, have to wear a mask. Everyone who enters the room itself, in fact, - and there are many who do in the course of an operation - must wear a mask, and the circulating nurse will absolutely make sure you do...or else. When everything goes well in an operating room, it can be as efficient and seamless as a finely calibrated Swiss timepiece. On this day, however, everything was not going well.

The surgery was very tricky, perhaps one of the most difficult surgeries to perform: a coronary artery bypass and aortic valve replacement. This is where the surgeon has to take arteries or veins from other parts of the body and place them in various places in the heart, bypassing the native diseased vessels. He also had to replace one of the valves which direct blood from the heart to the body. The patient was not very healthy to begin with, and his heart has already suffered a lot of damage from the massive heart attack he had a few days earlier.

Dr. Bryant, Robert W. Bryant, or "Dr. Bob" as he was known throughout the hospital, was barely able to control the enormous amount of bleeding that was taking place throughout the five-and-a-half hour surgery. Everywhere he placed his surgical instruments, blood would almost gush out of the area. The patient lost a lot of blood, and Dr. Bob had to give him a lot of blood products, along with multiple medicines to keep his blood pressure from plummeting. It was a very tense situation, and Dr. Bob was barely able to keep his cool. When the bleeding finally stopped, Dr. Bob went into a daze, which he has been doing more and more as of late, and stood at the operating table frozen for several minutes.

"Dr. Bryant?" asked the scrub nurse. "Dr. Bryant? Is something wrong?"

Dr. Bob was a junior attending cardiovascular surgeon, following in his father's footsteps. He was already accomplished - with a little help and prodding by his father - and was well on his way to becoming a prominent Chicago surgeon in his own right. He was very good at what he did, and he was a good person at heart, but as he worked his way through the grueling process that is medical school, residency (a surgical residency at that), and fellowship, he became more and more angry and bitter. He was always good at hiding this anger, but it was becoming more and more difficult as of late.

"Dr. Bob?" said the scrub nurse once again. "Is everything OK?"

Since Dr. Bob just stood there frozen, everyone thought it was time to "restart" the heart. Whenever bypass and/or valve surgery is performed, the heart is slowed down dramatically to facilitate operating on it. To keep the patient alive, blood is pumped into a cardiopulmonary bypass machine, a machine which pumps the life-giving and life-sustaining blood to the rest of the body. It is quite a large machine, with a lot of tubes going in and out, as well as multiple pumps that spin around endlessly. Putting a patient onto the machine is quite easy. Taking him or her off the machine, however, and "waking up" the heart can be particularly tricky, especially if the surgery has not gone as smoothly as one hopes. It is, perhaps, the most stressful time of the surgery because sometimes, the heart does not want to wake up.

"Dr. Bryant? Is it time to go off bypass? Shall we go ahead?" asked the perfusion therapist, the person who runs the cardiopulmonary bypass machine. The machine was situated not that far from the operating table. Dr. Bryant continued to stand there motionless for quite some time.

"Dr. Bryant?" asked the perfusion therapist again.

Dr. Bob did not answer or move, and he would have seemed as a statue had he not kept sniffing every once in a while. He always said it was his "hay fever acting up," but he always seemed to have shaky hands, watery eyes, and a runny nose all year long, even when not in hay fever season.

Everyone started to look at each other in awkward concern, wondering what was wrong with Dr. Bob. The fellow dared not ask Dr. Bob what was wrong as he was liable to chew his head off, something Dr. Bob has been doing more often as of late. The resident and medical student, basically, never talk to the attending surgeon.

"Dr. Bob?" snapped the scrub nurse. "What's wrong with you, sir?"

Dr. Bob gave another deep sniff and came out of his trance in a fit of rage, turning his eyes and angrily fixing them on the scrub nurse, Mary, who was not afraid of any of the doctors, something borne out of her many years of experience at Chicago Memorial Hospital. She even stood up to L. William Bryant himself, to the amazement of the nurses and the horror of the other doctors. When he backed down, Mary was forever a hero and legend in the Department of Surgery.

"Who the hell do you think you're talking to?" yelled Dr. Bob.

"You! You're just standing there like a statue, while the patient is on the table!" Mary yelled back. Everyone else stood frozen in fear.

"I am in charge here! I do whatever the hell I want!" screamed back Dr. Bob, and with that, he took the needle forceps in his hand - with needle still attached - and stabbed Mary in her hand. Mary screamed out in pain, and Dr. Bob stood frozen for a moment, with the gravity of what he just did slowly sinking in, and he stormed out of the operating room without saying a word or looking at anyone.

"Oh my God!" screamed the circulating nurse, Kelly. "Mary, are you alright?"

Mary took off her sterile glove to see if the needle had penetrated her skin. It had, and a small stream of blood was dripping down the back of her hand onto the tray table, on all those neatly arranged, and heretofore sterile, surgical tools.

Crying, Mary said, "That son of a bitch," and she left the room. Kelly tried to go with her, but Mary stopped her.

"Stay here and help finish the operation. The patient needs to go back on bypass," said Mary, holding her stabbed hand close to her body. "You!" she screamed to the senior cardiovascular surgery fellow, "Finish this case."

The fellow, Dr. James, who is finishing up his fellowship this year and already had a job lined up in suburban Los Angeles, took over.

"We're ready to go back on bypass," he said to the perfusion therapist. The patient's heart started up without incident, and Dr. James finished the case, with the senior resident and medical student helping him as best they could. No one made a sound throughout the rest of the operation. The only sound that could be heard in that operating room was the rhythmic beeping of the oxygen monitor.

4

The room was as dark as a moonless night in the Arabian desert. The silence of the call room at the hospital was piercing. Dr. Bob's sniffing, interestingly enough, had calmed down just enough to allow him to take a few moments of well-deserved sleep. He had been working very hard the last few weeks. The clinical service was very busy, and he had been doing about two heart operations a day. Add to that a very sick group of patients in the intensive care unit, and Dr. Bob quickly became exhausted, both physically and mentally. That was despite having a full contingent of medical students, residents, and fellows.

Dr. Bob's physical exhaustion was readily apparent, and it was easy to understand why. Yet, it was his mental exhaustion that was most taxing on him. And at first glance, one would wonder why he would be so mentally strained. He was an excellent surgeon and clinician. His teaching skills were widely acclaimed, and he would win Teacher of the Year almost every year since he became an attending surgeon. The burden on his mind, however, became heavier with the passing of time, and having to carry this burden day in and day out is what made him bitter and angry.

He never wanted to be a doctor. He hated the sight of blood. He had wanted to be a writer, and he was an excellent writer very early in his life. Writing was his passion. But his "hot-shot" father would not hear it. *Robert W. Bryant would be a surgeon and that's that.* So, he went along, figuring that he would eventually like it, and his father's position at Chicago Memorial Hospital would not hurt his prospects at becoming successful, either.

Yet, the younger Bryant never liked it. In fact, he hated his profession more and more as time passed. Since his father was so invested in his career, however, he felt obligated to play the role of the faithful son, especially since his sister ran away from home when she was 15. He never forgave her for that. He became a doctor, in his mind, to compensate for his sister's failings.

He was in the very deepest of sleep when his pager went off. Dr. Bob ignored the musical chime. A few minutes passed, and the pager went off again. He ignored it again. Yet, the person paging him was persistent, not dissuaded by Dr. Bob's continued stubbornness. Every few minutes or so, the pager would calmly go off. The message on the pager was always the same: "Duplicate Message: 45324."

Those five numbers were the hospital extension at which the person paging him was, with increasing impatience, waiting for his call. The only difference between each message was the time stamp. Finally, Dr. Bob's fog of sleep gave way to another fit of rage, and he practically jumped out of the bed and turned on the light. His shaking hands reached for the phone and dialed the number on the pager.

Dr. Bob screamed curses into the phone, and the curses came right back at him. Dr. Bob was taken aback by the response, finally realizing who it was: Dr. Brian Frank. He was the program director of the Cardiovascular Surgery fellowship. He was his direct boss, and the man slated to become chair of surgery when Dr. Bryant the elder eventually retires (or dies). Dr. Frank has never liked Dr. Bob's father. He never liked his heavy-handed tactics, and he also resented his success. He also resented how blatantly he helped his son elevate in the ranks of the surgical residency and fellowship. So, he made it his job to keep Dr. Bryant the son as honest as possible, a job he thoroughly enjoyed.

Dr. Bob got up and left the room and started to walk towards Dr. Frank's office, which was in another building on the hospital campus. Word had quickly spread about how he stabbed Mary, and as he walked the halls of the patient unit, all the staff looked at Dr. Bob in angered astonishment. For his part, looked no one in the face, walking to Dr. Frank's office with his eyes to the floor practically the entire time.

He approached the secretary's desk and, with a very

somber look, she told him, "You can go right in, doctor. He is waiting to see you."

"Thank you," Dr. Bob said.

He opened the door to the office, all lined with mahogany and Dr. Frank's various degrees and certificates, and immediately sat down on a plush leather chair in front of Dr. Frank's mahogany desk.

"What was that?" Dr. Frank nearly screamed across the desk.

"What was what?" retorted Dr. Bob, sniffing his nose and wiping away some clear secretions.

"Don't act flip with me," Dr. Frank screamed again, louder this time. He was about to scream at him again until his pager went off. He turned to look at the number, his face becoming even more red than before. He then gave Dr. Bob a harsh scowl as he picked up the phone and dialed.

"Yeah, what do you want," he said with scorn. "He's right here. We're having a meeting, and we're..."

An unintelligible scream was heard on the receiver which interrupted Dr. Frank.

"Alright, alright. He's on the way." Dr. Frank slammed down the phone.

"Your father is asking to see you in his office," Dr. Frank said, looking a bit dejected but still very angry.

Dr. Bob, now smirking, got up and turned toward the door, wiping his nose. Dr. Frank grabbed him tightly by the arm and pulled him closer to him.

"Let me go," quipped Dr. Bob, with disgust on his face.

"One day, you spoiled *shit*, daddy won't be here to save your ass. And believe you me, I'll be there to ride you like a Harley," Dr. Frank whispered in a low voice.

"Can't wait," said Dr. Bob with a blank but triumphant face, and with that, Dr. Frank let go of his arm and nearly pushed him out of his office. Dr. Bob gave a sly smirk to Dr. Frank and walked out of the office. Dr. Frank's anger could hardly be contained as he sat in his chair, and it caused him to tremble. After a few moments, he slammed his desk with his fist.

Dr. Bryant the elder's office was not that far away from Dr. Frank's office, so it did not take the son very long to make it to his father's office. As he was walking, he had a surgical instrument in his hand, and he was continually clicking it closed and reopening it with his hands. It was another nervous habit of his, picked up during his surgical residency and fellowship.

His father's office was even more luxurious than Dr. Frank's. The view of the city was immaculate, as was the mahogany walls and mahogany desk. Pictures of his family and colleagues were all over the wall, along with Dr. Bryant the elder's numerous certificates and awards. Dr. Bryant, the son, was in many of the family pictures, but, interestingly, not once was he smiling.

"What in God's name did you do?" his father yelled across the room to his son. His chair was facing the view of the city, and he yelled these words as soon as he heard his office door close.

"What possessed you to stick a dirty needle into her hand?"

Dr. Bryant, the son, stood there motionless, sniffing every so often and opening and closing the surgical instrument in his hand. He did not answer his father's angry inquiries.

"Bobby!" his father yelled again. "Answer me!"

That word, "Bobby," seemed to arouse the son from a trance-like state. His eyes then flashed with anger at his father. The surgical instrument broke in his hand, and realizing this, he dropped it to the floor.

"Don't...call...me...Bobby," Dr. Bryant, the son, said with a controlled rage. "My name is Robert." He hated when his father called him "Bobby." He felt belittled whenever his father would call him that name. He felt belittled by his father his entire life.

"Why did you stick Mary with a needle? The patient has HIV! Mary has to take post-exposure prophylaxis medications, and she will be gone for several weeks, if not forever. She is the best nurse this institution has ever had. What's wrong with you?" said Dr. Bryant the father.

"I...I don't know. I don't know why I did that," said the son, looking out blankly into space.

"Well, this is a very serious infraction. I have covered your ass so many times in the past, but this time, I can't help you. I am suspending you from clinical duty," declared the father.

"What? You can't do that! I have two more cases this morning and then rounds afterwards. You can't do that!" said the son, angrily.

"Hell I can't," said the father. "I have to maintain an image of integrity in this hospital. If I let this serious incident pass without any consequences to you, what will the people say? What will I look like? You are suspended immediately."

"Integrity..." says the son, chuckling sarcastically and looking away from his father.

"Yes, integrity," his father retorts.

"You can't do that! I am in charge..."

His father interrupted him, "No, *I* am in charge here!"

He walks up and stands right in his son's face.

"*I* am in charge here, *boy*. And don't you ever forget

it...Bobby," he says menacingly. He always knew how to push his son's buttons. The son trembles in fury, but says nothing.

"I am taking over your cases the rest of this week. Besides, you need the rest. You look like shit."

"Don't tell me what I need or do not need, you...," his son quipped back at him, unable to finish the sentence out of sheer fury. He then turned and left the office.

"Hey! Come back here!" the father yelled.

His son didn't look back.

"Robert!"

The door slammed hard behind Dr. Bob. The father sat in his chair and contemplated over what just transpired. He then picked up the phone and called the operating room.

"Hello, this is Dr. Bryant. Please take my son off the OR schedule and put my name in his place. He is no longer doing any cases for the time being."

Dr. Bob left the hospital after the meeting with his father. No one saw or heard from him the rest of the day.

5

The stillness of the dark was all at once disrupted by the piercing, high-pitched blare of the pager that was sitting on the night stand next to the bed. A hand reached over to the pager, grabbed it, and brought the pager closer to look at the number.

"Baby...baby," said the young female voice wiping away sleep from her eyes. "It's your home number. I think it's your wife."

The man, who woke up with a bit of a start, also wiped the sleep from his eyes and said, "Who?"

"I think it's your wife Dr. Bryant. You should answer it before she gets upset...or suspicious," said the nurse, Susan Montgomery.

"Yeah, right! She is in her own world all the time,"

Dr. Bryant, the father, said as he turned toward the lamp and turned the light on so he could see the phone to dial his home number. They were both under the cover laying next to each other in a small, yet comfortable, bed in a not-widely-known "on-call room" in the hospital. Normally, physicians who are on call will use one of these rooms to sleep while on duty. Sometimes, however, these rooms are used for other, not strictly medical, duties.

"Hello?" said Dr. Bryant. He had an arrogant smirk on his face, looking at his mistress as he spoke to his wife.

"Hello? Honey it's Anne. Why haven't you called me all day?" asked Mrs. Anne Bryant, Dr. Bryant's wife of 25 years. She was speaking like a young daughter to her father. "Have you forgotten what day today is?"

"Of course not, my love, of course not. How could I forget the anniversary of the day in which I married my one true love? I have just been so busy today. I had to do some unplanned cases today, so I have been swamped here at work. I'm sorry, dear," said Dr. Bryant, trying to quietly fight off the advances of Susan laying right next to him.

He covers the receiver so his oblivious wife can't hear and playfully whispers with a smile, "Stop it!"

Mrs. Bryant was sitting in his office at their estate-style home in the extremely affluent Chicago North Shore. The house, with seven bedrooms and eight bathrooms, was enormous, sitting on a hill with Lake

Michigan at its back. They had their own private beach at the bottom of the hill overlooking the lake.

The den was as stately inside as the home was outside. The walls were all mahogany, as was the large desk at which she was sitting on the phone talking to her husband. As his office at the hospital, the wall was lined with his certificates and awards along with many, many family pictures. Again, just as at the hospital, their son was not smiling in any of them.

Mrs. Bryant was fingering her wool-white hair while talking to him on the phone. She was dressed, as always, in the most expensive of clothing and jewelry: she was wearing a beautiful gown by Oscar De La Renta, worthy of the Academy Awards. She had a brilliant diamond wedding ring, and it was complemented by huge diamond earrings and an equally stunning diamond necklace.

Cardiovascular surgery was very good to Dr. Bryant, and he was equally very good to his wife. There was nothing she wanted that he did not provide for her. She came from a tough upbringing, and Dr. Bryant made sure her every wish was his command. It kept her happy and largely oblivious to what else was happening in the world around her. And this suited the good doctor just fine.

"Honey, what time is the awards ceremony? I don't want to miss that," inquired Mrs. Bryant.

"Five-thiry, honey. Then the reception is afterwards, and then we will go out to dinner." replied Dr. Bryant Jr.

"It's almost four, dear. When do you think I should leave?" asked Mrs. Bryant.

"Oh, honey, I think you should leave now. Call the driver and have him take you now. The way traffic is at this time of day, you will barely make it on time. I don't want you to miss the ceremony, baby," said Dr. Bryant.

"All right, dear. I am leaving now. I'll see you in a bit, dear," said Mrs. Bryant.

"Ok, my love, I will see you soon. I love you," said Dr. Bryant.

"I love you too, honey," said Mrs. Bryant, and then she hung up. She sat there at the desk thinking about her husband for a moment, and then she looked around at the den and peered outside through the large window into the well-manicured lawn and beautiful neighborhood in which they resided. All she could do was smile. She then picked up the phone and dialed an extension.

"Mr. Collins, I am ready to be driven to the city now," she said.

"My pleasure, ma'am. The car is ready for you," said Mr. Collins, their personal driver.

With that, she got up, walked out of the den and into the main foyer of their grand home. Looking into the foyer from the large, solid wood door - custom made in Italy - there was a grand marble staircase that wound around from right to left, encircling the round foyer. In the center of the foyer hung an enormous metal chandelier. The floor was an exquisite marble as well, the finest material money could buy. She walked out of the house and into the front driveway where Mr. Collins was waiting holding open the back door of the Bentley they owned.

"Thank you, Mr. Collins," she said.

Bowing, Mr. Collins replied, "My pleasure, ma'am." He closed the door and got in the driver's seat and started pulling away from the home. The gate enclosing the winding driveway leading to their home opened automatically, and he turned left toward the exit of their gated community.

"Going out to dinner with Dr. Bryant, ma'am?" asked Mr. Collins, looking at Mrs. Bryant fixing her hair in a vanity mirror in front of her.

"Later on. First, I am going to accompany William to a ceremony in his honor at the hospital. So, we're going to the hospital now, Mr. Collins," said Mrs. Bryant.

"Absolutely, ma'am. Hopefully, traffic won't be that bad," he said.

"I hope not. I really don't want to miss the ceremony," said Mrs. Bryant, looking a little worried.

"You won't, Mrs. Bryant, you won't," said Mr. Collins,

confidently.

He slowly passed the guard post at the front of their gated community and opened the window to talk to the guard.

"Afternoon Bob," said Mr. Collins.

"Hey there George," said Bob Johnson, the guard at the gate of the community. "Out to dinner again?"

"Yep, but not before Dr. Bryant gets some sort of award at the hospital," said Mr. Collins.

"So, I'll take it you will be coming back late, tonight?" asked Mr. Johnson.

"Oh yeah, just like always," said Mr. Collins.

Bob Johnson chuckled as he pressed the button to open the gate.

"Have a nice evening, bro," said Bob. "You have a great evening Mrs. Bryant," Bob yelled.

"Thank you, Bob," said Mrs. Bryant.

With that, Mr. Collins turned right out of the community and sped away toward the hospital. It would take them 45 minutes to get there.

Meanwhile, Dr. Bryant was getting dressed after another brief stint of lovemaking.

"You're not inviting me to dinner?" asked Susan, one of the younger ICU nurses who worked at the hospital, who was also getting dressed. Susan, unbeknownst to her, was just the latest of Dr. Bryant's "interns," as he liked to call them.

"Shut up and finish getting dressed, Susan," said Dr. Bryant slightly chuckling, but at the end of his laugh, and out of sight of Susan, a look of intense pain flashed across his face, and he stared across the call room for a few moments, pausing what he was doing.

"Hey, you OK? Was I that good?" smiled Susan.

"Wonderful, my dear, wonderful," said Dr. Bryant smiling and coming back to his senses.

Susan had finished getting dressed - she was in scrubs for work - and started towards the door.

"I'll see you later, Dr. Bryant," she said. She stopped and turned back to give him one last kiss.

"You coming to the reception?" he asked.

"Can't. I have spent all my breaks and lunch time here with you," Susan said smiling.

"Try to make it, if only for a few moments."

"But, won't you be with your wife?" Susan asked.

"Sure. You'll get to meet her, and I will get to see you again."

"I'll see what I can do," Susan said, looking a bit perplexed at his wanting his mistress to meet his wife. She then turned to leave the call room.

Dr. Bryant paused for a moment and decided to take a shower to clean himself off, just in case any trace of what had transpired could be detected by his wife, as unlikely as that possibility will be. There was a bathroom with a shower conveniently located in the call room. As he was taking a shower, all the preparations for the ceremony were being completed, and people already began to show up. It was a big day for Dr. Bryant, and he was relishing every moment of it as he cleaned himself off in the shower.

6

She woke up with a start, sweating profusely and breathing heavily. She looked around her to see where she was.

"Ma'am?" a flight attendant asked, looking a bit concerned. "Can I help you? Is there something wrong?"

Sarah didn't answer.

"Ma'am? Are you OK? Can I get you something to drink?" asked the flight attendant once again. The roar of the plane's engines permeated everything around them, and Sarah could barely hear the attendant talking to her. Suddenly, however, Sarah regained her composure.

"No, no, thank you. I am ok. I just had a bad dream,

that's all," Sarah said, looking a bit embarrassed at the amount of sweat that was pouring down her face. The flight attendant happened to have a napkin in her hand and gave it to her.

"Thank you very much," Sarah thankfully replied.

"We're about to land, so if you could secure your tray table, I would appreciate it," smiled the attendant.

"Yes, of course," Sarah said, complying immediately. Sarah was grateful that she did not scream out like she normally does when she has dreams of the sort she was having on the plane. When she came to grips with the fact that she was almost in Chicago; when she realized that she is finally going to face the thing from which she was running for so long, her heart began to race almost uncontrollably. The sweat continued to pour down her face, and she looked frantically around the plane, trying not to arouse any suspicion. Her hands were shaking, and she kept nervously fumbling her wedding ring. She fought hard not to burst out sobbing right then and there.

Within a few minutes, the plane made its bumpy descent and landed at Chicago's O'Hare International Airport.

"Ladies and Gentleman, we would like to welcome you to Chicago's O'Hare International Airport," the kind voice over the plane's interior loudspeaker said.

"If Chicago is your final destination, we would like to welcome you home."

As the flight attendant went on to list the various gates from where connecting flights will be taking off, Sarah ruminated over those words: *We would like to welcome you home.* This place was never home for her; it was a place of pain, of torment, of suffering, of despair. Home is none of these things, even if that is the only place one has ever been. She sat thinking about all the pain that "home" had caused her until she was the last passenger left on the plane. The look of panic on her face subsided a bit as she sat there, thinking about home.

"Ma'am? It is time to deplane," said the very same flight attendant. Her name was also Sarah. "Is there something wrong, ma'am? I have been watching you for a while, and I am concerned. Can I help you in any way?"

"No, thank you," said Sarah, grateful for the woman's concern. "I am quite all right. I am not feeling very well, and I am anxious to get to my hotel room and rest." This was a lie: actually, she was anxious to go back home to Seattle, her *real* home.

"Where are you staying?" asked the flight attendant.

"Right here at the Hyatt, next to the airport," said Sarah. Being right next to the airport where theoretically she could leave at any time, comforted her immensely.

"Do you need help with your bags?" asked the flight attendant of the same name.

"Oh no, I'm quite alright," said Sarah standing up finally. "I'll be fine."

With that, she opened up the overhead bin where her carry-on bag was and took it out. She then walked off the plane with the flight attendant behind her. The captain and other crew members were already off the plane.

"You take care, OK?" said the flight attendant.

"I will. Thank you very much for your concern," said Sarah. She walked through the walkway to the main terminal at O'Hare. The walk to the hotel was not very long, and before she knew it, she was at the front desk.

"Checking in, please," Sarah said to the front desk employee.

"Name, please?" said the employee.

"Sarah Bryan...Sarah Meyers, I mean," she said with a nervous laugh. "I just got married...it's kinda weird using my new name, I am not used to it."

"Yeah, I know. I just got married, too. Are you on your honeymoon?" said the front desk employee.

"No, no, no. I am here on personal business," said Sarah, eyes tearing up as she thought of what she was about to do.

"Mrs. Meyers, are you alright?" asked the employee, a little concerned. She handed Sarah a tissue.

"I'm fine," said Sarah, wiping her nose. "I'm fine. Can I get to my room, please?"

"Absolutely, ma'am. You are in room 345. Here is your room key. Please sign here."

Sarah quickly signed the hotel sign in sheet and grabbed her room key just as quickly. She found her way to room 345 and entered into the room. She nearly collapsed on the bed and started crying, and, with her hands violently shaking, she pulled out her cell phone and called her husband, Jonathan.

"Hello?" said Jonathan, immediately knowing who was on the other end. "Sarah? Baby? What's wrong? Where are you? Are you ok?" he asked frantically.

"I'm fine, I'm fine. I'm here in Chicago," Sarah said sniffing, feeling a little better after hearing Jonathan's voice. "I just arrived, and I'm in the hotel...I can't do this, Jonathan. I just can't do it."

"Hey, it's ok, baby. It's ok. You can do it, honey. You have been preparing for this a long time. You can do it. You have a strength in you that even you do not realize, babe," said Jonathan in his characteristic soothing voice. It made Sarah feel even better.

"I wanna come home," said Sarah, still sniffing.

"You will very soon, honey. Just do what you have to do and come home. I will be here waiting for you with open arms, my love," said Jonathan.

Sarah asked her husband, "Sing to me. Like you did when you proposed to me."

There was a long pause on the other line.

"Please, baby. Please."

Jonathan's eyes began to well up with tears, and he began to sing to his wife:

"Hey there, my beautiful. The sun shines in your eyes. Hey there, my beautiful. My heart melts with your smile. Hey there, my wonderful. I love all that is you. Hey there, my wonderful. My love for you is so true…"

Sarah closed her eyes and listened to her husband sing to her from thousands of miles away. She quickly fell asleep.

"Baby?" asked Jonathan. When there was no answer, he knew she was asleep and he hung up. He then sat there at his bed crying, longing for his wife to come home.

7

"And now, without further a due, let me call up to the podium, the guest of honor, Dr. L. William Bryant."

Dr. Frank strained ever so hard to feign a feeling of happiness and joy at the honoring of his colleague. As Dr. Bryant came up to the podium to address the large crowd assembled and having dinner, Dr. Frank reached out and was barely able to shake Dr. Bryant's hand. The rest of the banquet hall stood up in standing ovation, and Dr. Bryant looked out into the crowd at his colleagues, his loving wife, standing at the front table marked "Reserved," and he even managed to get a wink in to his mistress, who was sitting several tables back, smiling at him as well. No one noticed to whom the wink was addressed.

As he gave his speech, thanking his colleagues in the midst of it, everyone was busy eating their appetizers and trying to listen to the speech at the same time. There were butlers all over the room with trays and trays of tasty things to eat. The drinks from the open bar were also awash in the room, as well. Dr. Bryant ended his speech with this statement, "And I would be terribly unjust and horribly ungrateful, if I did not take the time to specifically thank and honor my beautiful, loving wife of 25 years, Mrs. Anne Bryant. In fact, today is our 25th wedding anniversary," and with that a collective gasp raised in the banquet hall, followed by applause.

Dr. Bryant, speaking over the applause, continued, "Without her, I would not be here today. Please, honey, stand up for everyone to see your beautiful face. Please, Anne, stand up."

Mrs. Bryant reluctantly stood up, looking embarrassed, yet smiling nonetheless, at everyone who stood to give her a standing ovation. Deep down, despite the look of bashfulness, she reveled in the attention. She always did love attention. Amidst the chaos of the standing ovation, Dr. Bryant was able to give another wink to his mistress.

Dr. Frank looks over at Dr. Bryant and his mistress, and his anger and frustration grows even more. He also glances at Mrs. Bryant with a look of scorn and a little pity. Yet, despite his anger and resentment at Dr. Bryant, Dr. Frank could not muster the courage to reveal Dr. Bryant's multiple affairs to Mrs. Bryant. Over the years, they have become friends, and he didn't want to destroy her nice and neat little world.

"And so," Dr. Bryant finished his speech, "you all will not mind if my beautiful wife and I leave this truly spectacular event a little early...we have dinner reservations to keep!"

The entire room burst into laughter then applause as Dr. Bryant walked back to his table. So many people come to their table to say their "hellos" and "congratulations," and he introduces each person to his nearly unceasingly smiling wife.

"Oh, honey, I want you to meet one of the best ICU nurses this hospital has," said Dr. Bryant, bringing Susan closer so she can meet his wife. Ms. Montgomery had long, golden hair that was nicely made despite her having worked a nearly 12 hour shift. Her face was full, but she was not overweight, fitting nicely in her hospital scrubs.

"Susan Montgomery. It is an honor to finally meet you Mrs. Bryant," said Susan as she moved closer to embrace Mrs. Bryant.

"Anne Bryant. The pleasure is mine," said Mrs. Bryant, who was totally oblivious to whom she was just embracing.

"Your husband always speaks very highly of you, and now that I see you, I can see why," said Susan, who made a quick glance to the widely smiling Dr. Bryant.

"Oh, he has always been very kind to me," said Mrs. Bryant, looking at her husband, who was holding a glass of champagne in his hand and beaming at his "prowess" at being able to stand together with his wife and mistress completely undetected.

"It is an honor to get to work with and know your husband, Mrs. Bryant. You have a very special man living with you," said Susan, looking at Dr. Bryant.

"Oh yes, I know, Ms. Montgomery, I know," said Mrs. Bryant, and she moved over and gave her husband a kiss on the cheek. This seemed to bother Susan, but she worked hard at hiding her feelings.

"I must be going, now. Mrs. Bryant. I've had a very long day, and I need to get home. It was such a pleasure to meet you."

"Likewise, my dear."

"Dr. Bryant, I will see you later, sir," said Susan to Dr. Bryant, in the most formal way possible.

"See you later, Susan," said Dr. Bryant.

"She is a very nice girl, isn't she honey?" said Mrs. Bryant to her husband, which interrupted his long glance Susan Montgomery as she walked out of the large reception room.

"Oh yes, darling, very nice."

"Is she married?"

"No, I do not think so," Dr. Bryant said, trying to look confused at her question.

"Wouldn't she be perfect for Bobby?" asked Mrs. Bryant, taking a sip of her drink.

"Yes, I think she would, honey," said Dr. Bryant with a smile.

"By the way, I haven't seen Bobby at all tonight. Where is he?" asked Mrs. Bryant with a bit of concern on her face.

"Frankly, I'm surprised he is not sitting with us at dinner."

"I have no idea. I haven't seen since this morning. He wasn't feeling very well today, and I actually did his cases for him. I'm sure he's fine," said Dr. Bryant, trying to reassure his wife's worry. He purposefully neglected to mention the needle incident.

More and more people kept coming up to the couple and saying their "hellos" and "congratulations," but when Dr. Bryant took a look at his watch, his eyes widened because they will be late for their dinner reservation if they stayed a moment longer.

"I'm sorry, everyone," Dr. Bryant told the crowd, "but we really must be going. It's our anniversary," stealing a smile to his wife as he said that.

They both started walking toward the door to leave.

"Dr. and Mrs. Bryant, everyone," said Dr. Frank on the microphone from the podium one more time. His smile could have been more fake.

Suddenly, Dr. Bryant turns pale and can't speak.

"Honey, honey? Bill, what's wrong?" said Mrs. Bryant. She became more frantic with every passing second he couldn't answer her questions.

"Bill? Bill? Answer me! Bill? Bill!"

He looked at her with a glazed look of nothingness, and he fell briskly to the ground and began convulsing. A collective gasp and numerous screams emanated from the hall, and Dr. Frank runs down from the podium to Dr. Bryant's side.

"Call a Code!" Dr. Frank screamed.

Several people scurried to the nearest phone to call a CODE BLUE. Dr. Frank held him as best as he could, preventing him from hurting himself. About 3 minutes later, an entourage of residents and nurses, a respiratory therapist and pharmacist arrived with a red tackle box with all the drugs and supplies necessary for when a patient's heart stops.

"Excuse me, Mrs. Bryant," said one of the team leaders, Dr. Joseph Sanders. He was a junior faculty member in the Department of Pulmonary/Critical Care Medicine, and he was the attending physician working that month in the Intensive Care Unit. Ignoring Mrs. Bryant's frantic screams, Dr. Sanders began working on Dr. Bryant alongside Dr. Frank. Just then, Susan came running into the hall and stopped dead in her tracks when she saw the convulsing Dr. Bryant on the floor. Yet, she mustered the ability to hold back her tears and took Mrs. Bryant into her arms, consoling her as best as possible.

"It's OK, Mrs. Bryant," said Susan, rubbing her shoulders. "They are taking good care of your husband."

As she turned to look at her still seizing lover, tears were streaming down her face.

8

"God damn it, stop seizing!" screamed Dr. Sanders.

Dr. Bryant is now in an intensive care unit room, with a number of healthcare personnel surrounding him.

He was lying, still seizing, in a hospital bed, eyes closed. In his mouth was a light blue cylindrical tube connected to darker blue tubing, which was connected to a ventilator to his left. They had already placed a number of IVs in his arms, and he had a special type of IV catheter in his right groin area.

Dr. Sanders was at the head of the bed, and around the bed were several nurses, residents, and the on call Pulmonary/Critical Care fellow, who was training to be a specialist like Dr. Sanders. They have already pumped a lot of medications to try to stop the seizures, but they are not working, to Dr. Sanders' enormous frustration.

"We've given him Ativan, Dilantin, and even propofol. Nothing is working," said Dr. Sanders. "You know what, I'll give him pentothal. His brain is probably already fried because he's been seizing non-stop for the last 60 minutes." Dr. Sanders was sort of talking to himself and to the staff in the room, who were frantically scurrying about getting various things set up in the room.

"Let's give him pentothal please," Dr. Sanders said to one of the nurses. She then left the ICU room and quickly came back with a syringe full of a clear liquid. She quickly injected it into Dr. Bryant's IV. After about 30-45 seconds, Dr. Bryant finally stopped seizing.

"It's about damn time," Dr. Sanders said with a sigh of angry relief. Almost without thinking he blurted out: "Let's get a whole set of labs: CBC, CMP, troponin, lactate, PT, PTT, blood culture, urine culture, and sputum culture." "Oh," he then interrupted himself looking as if he was awakened from a trance, "we also have to do an LP." Looking at a tall, thin, and younger doctor with short, black hair who had managed to stand right next to him, he asked, "Can you get that set up, Mohammed?"

Mohammad Ahmed, the Pulmonary/Critical Care fellow, nodded and then walked out of the room to get the supplies. The labs were all drawn, and by the time Dr. Ahmed came back, Dr. Sanders had calmed down enough to take a rest in the corner of the ICU room. The thick tension that was in the room a few minutes earlier lifted a little. Dr. Bryant was resting on the ventilator, not moving a muscle, because Dr. Sanders wanted him to be that way.

"We're ready, Dr. Sanders," said Dr. Ahmed.

The nurses helped turn Dr. Bryant on his side, and they were holding him there throughout the entire procedure. An "LP," is a lumbar puncture, or spinal tap.

"Oh...I almost forgot," said Dr. Sanders, looking into the air as he is getting dressed in a sterile gown and gloves. He already had a mask with a face shield on.

"We need a chest x-ray as soon as the LP is done. I want to make sure the tube is in good position."

"OK, Dr. Sanders," said one of the nurses, who walked out to give the orders to the unit secretary.

With one stick of the needle, clear fluid dripped out of the plastic end of the spinal needle. Dr. Sanders began to collect the fluid in several tubes.

"Normally I'd let you do it, Mohammed, but...you know..." said Dr. Sanders. Mohammed nodded.

"I totally understand..."

Dr. Sanders walked out of the room and went to the desk facing it and sat down, taking a big breath and rubbing his eyes He grabbed the chart and began to document the events of the past several hours on a computer directly in front of him. Dr. Ahmed walked out of the ICU room with the three bottles of spinal fluid and walked them to the lab for testing. Just then, the x-ray technician came with the portable x-ray machine to take a chest x-ray. As he is typing away, a familiar voice called out to him from the counter above his desk.

"Joe?"

Dr. Sanders looked up and saw Susan Montgomery.

"Oh, hey Susan! How are you?" said Dr. Sanders. His eyes brightened a bit, as he was very happy to see her. Although, with that joy came a twinge of pain.

They had actually dated for quite some time, and it was fast becoming serious. In fact, he had bought her engagement ring a few weeks back and formally proposed. She initially accepted his proposal, but then, suddenly, she broke off their relationship. He had tried to find out why multiple times, to no avail.

"I'm OK, just shocked about what has happened to Dr. Bryant," said Susan, her face swollen as if she had been crying a lot.

"Yeah, I know," said Dr. Sanders. "It took me one hour to get him to stop seizing. I hope his brain is not fried."

Susan did not like to hear that from him, and she showed it on her face.

"Hey? Are you OK? You look like you have been crying. Is…everything alright? Can I help with something?" He got up and walked over to her side, rubbing her shoulder. Susan went stiff with tension, and Dr. Sanders slowly backed off with a pained look of surprise on his face.

"Mrs. Bryant is going crazy with grief, and it's hard not to feel for her, you know? I've been trying to console her the whole time you were working on him," said Susan, looking away from her former lover.

"Oh wow. But, why are you even here?"

"I was having coffee when I heard the CODE BLUE called. So, I went to help. I actually came in here to see if Mrs. Bryant can see her husband now."

"Sure, she can come in. I actually need to speak with her."

"OK, Joe. Thanks," said Susan, turning and walking away.

"It was nice to see you," yelled Dr. Sanders. Susan didn't answer, and he had that same look of pained confusion.

A few moments later, she and Mrs. Bryant walked toward the ICU room. Mrs. Bryant was visibly shaken, and her makeup was all smeared from the endless tears she had been shedding for her very sick husband. Dr. Sanders got up to meet the both of them.

"Mrs. Bryant?" said Dr. Sanders. She was barely able to nod her response.

"I'm Joe Sanders, ICU attending. I am so sorry to have to meet you under these circumstances, ma'am, " said Dr. Sanders.

Mrs. Bryant was barely able to extend her hand to meet Dr. Sander's already extended hand. Mrs. Bryant gently nodded her head, tears welling up in her already blood-shot eyes. In a barely audible voice, she said, "How…," clearing her throat, "how's my husband?"

"He's very sick Mrs. Bryant," said Dr. Sanders his face suddenly very stern, but with compassion and empathy.

"May I see him now?" asked Mrs. Bryant.

"Yes, yes, of course," said Dr. Sanders, as he led both she and Susan into the ICU room. Mrs. Sanders froze in her place when she saw her husband with all these tubes and wires, connected to several IV poles and the ventilator. She began sobbing quietly, and Susan was hugging her close, trying to console her. Quietly, Dr. Sanders was telling Mrs. Bryant the events of the last few hours, and as he spoke, her sobbing only became more intense. She then went to the side of Dr. Bryant's bed and grabbed his hand, wiping her tears with her other hand.

"Bill, honey. I'm here, honey. I won't leave you, honey. I won't leave you," said Mrs. Bryant, as tears streamed down her already red and makeup-smeared cheeks. She began sobbing again.

"I'll leave you now, Mrs. Bryant. Please, do not hesitate to call me if you need anything. Here is my cell phone number. Call me anytime," said Dr. Sanders, writing down his cell phone number on the back of one of his business cards that he pulled out of his front pocket. He then handed her the card.

"Call me any time, Mrs. Bryant," said Dr. Sanders.

Mrs. Bryant looked up at Dr. Sanders, a look of appreciation in her eyes as she took the card. Susan continued rubbing her shoulders. Dr. Sanders then walked out of the room to continue his typing on the computer.

"Susan, you can go home now, dear. Thanks so very much for everything you have done. I want to be alone with my Bill now," said Mrs. Bryant, reaching her hand out and holding Susan's with a look of deep and profound gratitude.

"Are you sure? I can stay with you, it's no problem," said Susan.

"Oh no, dear. Please, go home and get some rest. My place is here," said Mrs. Bryant, with a very faint smile.

"OK, Mrs. Bryant. Please," said Susan taking the business card and writing down her cell phone number as well, "You can also call me if you need anything, as well. Call me any time."

"Thank you so very much, dear," said Mrs. Bryant. She then pulled up a chair and sat down next to her husband.

Susan turned to leave the ICU room. Although she could not say it, she so very wanted to spend the night by his bedside as well. And as she left the ICU room, tears were streaming down her face. Dr. Sanders, furiously typing away, did not notice that she left.

As Mrs. Bryant sat next to her husband, oblivious to the comings and goings of various nurses, residents, and other staff, she kept saying quietly through tears and sobs, "Please, Bill, please don't die."

And as Susan, crying as well, walked out of the ICU, she kept saying to herself, "Please, Bill, please don't die."

9

"Can I help you?" asked Bob Johnson, the gate attendant at the Bryants' exclusive, gated community.

"I am taking my passenger to the Bryant residence," said the cab driver, Mohammed Qureshi.

"Hmm, they did not tell me they were expecting any guests," said Mr. Johnson. "I'll have to phone the residence. May I ask who your passenger is?"

"Dr. Bryant's daughter," said Mr. Qureshi.

"Daughter?" asked Bob Johnson in a very confused voice. He quickly became suspicious, and he picked up the phone and dialed George Collins, who answered a few moments later.

"Hello? George?" said Bob Johnson. "How are ya,

bud? Listen...I have someone at the gate who says she is Dr. Bryant's daughter. I never knew he had a daughter. Should I let her go through?"

As the conversation between Bob Johnson and George Collins was continuing, Sarah Bryant's anxiety was at an all-time high. Throughout the entire cab ride to the house, she wanted to tell the cab driver to go back dozens of times. Yet, now, as they were held back at the gate, her determination to get to the house and face her past began to get stronger and stronger.

"Daughter?" asked George in utter amazement. "What does she look like?"

As Bob described her to George, George started to become weak in the knees, and he had to hold himself up on the kitchen counter.

"Oh my Lord...oh my Precious Lord..." said George Collins in utter astonishment.

Mr. Collins had been with the family for years, and wherever they went, he went. He watched Sarah grow up, and they had a very close relationship. She was the daughter he never had, he would always say. He was devastated when she ran away, being – of course – oblivious to the circumstances of her sudden departure.

"Hey Bob..." George's voice was breaking up, "ask...ask her what her favorite teddy bear's name was." Tears were streaming down George's face.

Bob was a bit surprised at the question, but he complied. He turned to the window and said, "Can she open her window?" Sarah was a bit confused at what was transpiring.

"The attendant is asking you to open your window, ma'am," said Mr. Qureshi. Sarah did so.

"Ma'am, I'm sorry about this, but the person at the Bryant residence is asking what the name of your favorite teddy bear was," said Bob Johnson.

Sarah was taken aback at this question, and all the horrible memories came rushing back into her consciousness. She started to cry profusely. Yet, she soon realized that only one person would have asked that question, and she managed to let out a quick smile, while still crying.

"Muf...Muffy..." and Sarah began to cry even more forcefully and she sat back in the seat, with her head in her hands.

Mr. Qureshi was astonished at this sudden burst of emotion on the part of Sarah.

"Ma'am," he said. "Ma'am, are you alright?"

Sarah did not answer him. She just continued to cry. Mohammed reached for the box of tissue in the passenger seat and reached back through the narrow opening in the plastic barrier between the front and back seat to hand her the box.

"Ma'am...ma'am," said Mr. Qureshi, at which time Sarah looked up, tears streaming down her face, and took the box of tissue.

"Thank you, sir," said Sarah.

Bob Johnson stood there frozen at what was transpiring. He could hear George sobbing on the telephone.

"What did she say, Bob?" asked George. Bob did not answer.

"Bob!" yelled George. "What did she say?"

"Uh...Muffy, George, Muffy."

"Oh my Precious Lord! Oh my Precious Lord! Let her come, let her come," said George.

George could not believe that Sarah was still alive and now here in Chicago. George ran to the front door, opened it, and ran to the side of the road in anticipation of the arrival of the taxi cab. He was an old man, and at the end of his run, he was breathing quite heavily. He did not care, though. He barely noticed his significant shortness of breath.

"Go ahead, sir," said Bob Johnson. He took one last look at Sarah as the cab drove past the gate.

The taxi pulled into the driveway of the Bryant house, and George nearly fell over himself getting to the door where Sarah was sitting. He opened the door, even before the taxi cab had come to a complete stop, and fell to his knees, sobbing in front of her. Sarah was crying as well, and Mr. Qureshi could hardly believe his eyes.

"My little Sarah! My little Sarah!"

George looked up at her, his eyes full of tears, and he pulled her out of the taxi and gave her a very long embrace.

"I can't believe it's you," he said, holding her head in his hands. Her eyes were full of tears as well.

"It's nice to see you again, George," said Sarah, smiling through her tears.

"You have come back to me from the dead, my little Sarah!"

George then pulled Sarah to his chest and embraced her as a father who has seen his daughter - thought to be dead - alive and well before him after more than a decade. He then pushed her away to take a look at her, to see what sort of woman she has become.

"You are even more beautiful than I imagined," said George. "You don't know how much I have wanted to see you again, Sarah. My precious little Sarah," and he hugged her again, almost not wanting to let her go.

Mr. Qureshi was crying at the sight of this emotional reunion. When George walked over to the driver's side to pay the cab driver, he noticed that he was crying.

"Is everything alright, sir?" asked George, wiping away his own tears.

"Yes..." said Mr. Qureshi crying, "seeing you two embrace reminded me of my own daughter. She died two years ago in a car accident. She was only 12."

"Oh my Precious Lord! I am so sorry for your loss Mr..." said George, as he handed the cab driver $100.

"Mohammed. Mohammed Qureshi," said the cab driver, and he became astonished as the sight of the $100 bill.

"I can't accept this, sir," said Mr. Qureshi. "This is too much, sir."

"Please," said George, "take it as a gift...a gift for giving me my Sarah back." George then walked to the back of the cab and pulled out Sarah's bags from the trunk, closing it afterwards.

"Is Sarah your daughter?" asked Mr. Qureshi.

"Oh no, she is the daughter of my employer," said George. Mr. Qureshi could not believe it.

"But, we were very close, and it has been so long since I have last seen Sarah," said George.

"Thank you very, very much sir," said Mr. Qureshi. He then backed up the taxi and drove away, wiping tears from his eyes as he remembered his own daugther, Fatima.

"I just want to hug you and never let you go, my Sarah. How are you?" said George.

"I'm fine, George," said Sarah.

"I am so happy you came back home. Where were you all these years?" said George.

"I am living in Seattle now, George. I just got married, and I wanted to come back and see my father. Is he home?"

"Oh my God!" exclaimed George. "I forgot all about your father, being overwhelmed by the happiness of your return." George's face turned from ecstatic joy to stern concern, "Sarah. Your father is very sick. He is in the hospital right now in intensive care. Your mother has been at his bedside ever since."

Sarah's strength melted away, and she began to cry. "What? When did this happen?"

"Last night," said George.

"Is he OK?" asked Sarah.

"I don't know. I haven't heard from your mother since she sent me home last night from the hospital," said George.

Sarah could not believe what she was hearing. "I need

to see him right away!" said Sarah.

"Uh...yes...absolutely," said George. "I will take you to the hospital right away." George quickly put her bags inside the house and came out of the garage with one of the family's many S-Class Sedans. As Sarah waited, she looked around at the neighborhood, with tears streaming down her face. Even though it was a relatively warm morning, she felt cold, and she was shivering a bit.

"You feeling sick, Sarah?" asked George as he opened the door for her, noticing that she was shivering.

"No, I'm just nervous and scared that's all," said Sarah.

"I will take you to the hospital as fast as possible, Sarah. Your mother is still there. She will be so happy to see you!" said George, who was so excited to have Sarah back home. Sarah got into the car, and he backed out of the driveway and quickly started out of the neighborhood on his way to the hospital. As they drove toward the city, George kept trying to make conversation, noticing how nervous Sarah was, but she didn't want to talk. So, they remained silent the entire trip to Chicago Memorial Hospital.

10

The ICU is a noisy place. There are residents, fellows, medical students, nurses, technicians, clerical staff, x-ray technicians, and other clinical services that pass through at some time throughout a typical day. The noise is not very conducive to healing, but no matter how much the staff tries, the constant hum of feet, chatter, x-ray machines, and the like permeate each room of the ICU. The medical intensive care unit of Chicago Memorial Hospital is quite big, with 24 rooms laid out in a big square. In the middle of the square is the nurses' station, conference area, and computer stations for the staff to use. Dr. Bryant's room was near the middle of the square. A large collection of people were walking toward his room: it was the ICU team on their morning rounds.

The ICU team consists of the attending physician, Dr. Joseph Sanders; the fellow Dr. Mohammed Ahmed;

four interns, who are first year residents just recently graduated from medical school; two senior residents, who are further along in their training than the interns; nurses, and other staff, such as a pharmacist and a nutritionist. Morning rounds usually start at about 7:30 A.M., and they can last all morning, especially if the ICU is full, which it was at this current time. Dr. Bryant was next on their trek through the ICU.

"Bed 7," said the intern assigned to Dr. Bryant. He was quite nervous, as his patient was a major VIP. He really should not have been, because if anything were to go wrong, the responsibility (and the heat) would fall on the senior resident working with the intern. In reality, however, the ultimate responsibility would fall on the attending physician, and Dr. Sanders took this responsibility quite seriously, for all his patients, not just his VIP patients. Since Chicago Memorial was quite prominent, it had VIP patients all the time.

"This is a 56 year-old white..."

"Hold on," interrupted Dr. Sanders. The intern looked at his attending with a nervous eye. "His race is irrelevant to me, and I want you guys to understand this. We have been trained, traditionally, to mention the race of our patients. I don't like this. If his race is relevant to the disease process, I will ask for it. Our patients are men or women, that's it. I want you guys to pound this into your heads. Go ahead, Mike."

"56 year-old *man*," looking at Dr. Sanders, "who

developed sudden onset seizures last night. He quickly progressed to status epilepticus, and he seized for at least 60 minutes. He only stopped after pentothal was given. He was intubated before coming to ICU. He has been stable since, only seizing a few times only briefly. He is on a propofol drip for the seizures."

The intern looked at Dr. Sanders to see if he could continue. Dr. Sanders frequently interrupted his intern presentations to make a pertinent teaching point. Except for his sermon about race, which he could not resist, Dr. Sanders was silent today, listening intently to the presentation. He was deep in thought, contemplating over Dr. Bryant's case. He lost quite a bit of sleep over Dr. Bryant thinking about why such a healthy man would suddenly become so sick. By the time the morning came around, however, everything became quite clear.

"Go ahead Mike," said Dr. Sanders, prodding him to continue.

"His past medical history is otherwise unremarkable except for essential hypertension. No past surgical history, and no known drug allergies. The only medication he was taking was metoprolol. His family history is negative. Social history is positive for tobacco use; he smoked 2 packs a day for the past 30 years. Social alcohol, no illicits. I could not get a review of systems because he was already intubated before he came to the ICU."

The intern looked visibly tired as he was

presenting Dr. Bryant's case: he had been up all night taking care of him along with the resident and fellow. The intern then went over the laboratory results, many of which were abnormal and were a result of his repeated seizures. He next talked about the radiology results.

"Chest xray showed numerous nodules on both lungs, along with what appears to be a large left hilar mass. This was confirmed on CT of the chest, and in addition he has large, bulky adenopathy in bilateral hila. The CT of the brain also shows numerous lesions that look quite consistent with mets. Oh, the adrenals also looked like they had masses on them. So, in summary, this is a 56 year old man with status epilepticus, respiratory failure, and what appears to be metastatic lung cancer."

The group was hushed when they heard this terrible news. Dr. Sanders was still in intent thought when he seemed to suddenly "snap out" of his trance and ask the intern, "So, what is the treatment plan?"

"Plan is to keep him on the vent and heavily sedated. The cultures are all negative so far. Oncology will be called today to see if anything can be done for him."

"I am not sure much *can* be done for him, frankly," said Dr. Sanders. "This is a very unfortunate situation. I am not sure how much meaningful neurologic recovery he will have. I will need to discuss the findings with his wife. Mohammed, take the team ahead on rounds and we will touch base later..."

"Uh, excuse me, Dr. Sanders?" interrupted the intern, Mike.

"Yes," replied Dr. Sanders, a bit surprised.

"Did we discuss code status with the family?"

The entire team was taken aback by the boldness of the suggestion, most especially Dr. Sanders. "Code status" is medical jargon for the decision someone has made in case his or her heart or breathing stops. Normally, when this happens, a "code blue" is called, and emergency CPR, shocks, and medications are given in an attempt to revive the heart. Most often, a breathing tube is inserted in the trachea, or wind pipe, to assist in breathing. The default position is a "full code," which means do everything possible to keep the heart beating in case it stops.

Some people elect not to have such heroic measures at the end of life, for whatever reason. These people typically sign a "do not resuscitate," or "DNR," order instructing the medical staff not to intervene in case the heart or breathing stops. Some people have this stipulated in a "living will," which is a document a person signs, while they are alive and well, instructing what to be done in case of terminal illness or cardiac arrest. Many people do not have this issue addressed, and Dr. Bryant was no different.

One would have thought that a doctor such as Dr. Bryant, having seen such end of life situations innumerable times in his career, would have had his end of life wishes addressed. But, he always felt alive and invincible. It never occurred to him, never even crossed his mind once, that he would one day be in an intensive care unit, on a ventilator, fighting for his life against terminal cancer.

Dr. Sanders, on the other hand, already had his end of life wishes spelled out: if he is terminal, he wants to be *not* resuscitated. *If I am terminal,* he would always say, *then leave me alone and let me meet my Maker.*

"No, Mike, I did not discuss code status with the family. And by the way, I think it is very inappropriate for you to discuss such things with patients or their families. Such a discussion should ideally come from the primary attending, not an ICU intern. Don't worry, though, I will bring it up, OK? Is that satisfactory to you?"

Dr. Sanders was visibly annoyed and angered by the intern's comments. Mike seemed to retreat into his skin, and he started to sweat profusely. "I'm...I'm...I'm sorry Dr. Sanders," he said timidly.

Dr. Sanders did not reply; he did not even look at the intern.

"Keep rounding, guys," said Dr. Sanders, the quip in his voice declared to the world his extreme disapproval at the intern's question. Mike meant no harm; he was trying to be complete, trying to impress Dr. Sanders. It backfired miserably.

As the ICU team moved to the next room, Dr.

Sanders walked into Dr. Bryant's ICU room. Mrs. Bryant was sitting at his bedside, holding her husband's hand, quietly praying to herself. In between her prayers, she would nod off. She did not move since the night before, and she was visibly exhausted.

"Mrs. Bryant? Ma'am, have you been here the whole night?" asked Dr. Sanders, a bit concerned for her.

"Yes," said Mrs. Bryant, her face still smeared from the tears. "I can't bear to leave his side."

Dr. Sanders pulled up a chair to sit next to her, and he reached over and rubbed her shoulder gently.

"Have you been updated on your husband's case?" asked Dr. Sanders.

Her demeanor lightened a bit as she said, "No. How is he doing?" asked Mrs. Bryant.

She had hope that her husband would walk out of the ICU. Dr. Sanders knew - almost for a fact - that Dr. Bryant would not even wake up from his coma. Breaking bad news is perhaps the most difficult thing for a doctor to do. Frequently, neither the patient nor their anxious family wants to hear the bad news, and many times, it is difficult to gauge the ability of the patient or family to take the bad news. This is especially true in situations of critical illness such as this. Yet, Dr. Sanders has done this enough times, unfortunately, to be half-way decent at it.

Now, Dr. Sanders did not have the heart to overwhelm Mrs. Bryant with the awful news of his widely spread cancer, but he felt that he had to tell her everything he knew. He realized this may be too much for her to handle, but given the circumstances of Dr. Bryant's illness, he did not have the luxury of giving her the news piecemeal.

"He is still quite sick, ma'am," said Dr. Sanders. "For the most part, he has stopped seizing..."

"Well that's good news, right?" chimed in Mrs. Bryant. She was clinging to any shred of hope.

"Yes, yes, of course, but I am giving him strong doses of medicines to quiet his brain," said Dr. Sanders.

He really did not want to dash any hope she may have, because hope is all she has to rely on at this point, but at the same time, he did not want to give her false hope. That is another difficult balancing act for doctors taking care of critically ill patients: while you don't always want to be "Dr. Doom and Gloom," it is worse to give families hope knowing it is going to be dashed a few days or weeks later. That is nothing short of cruelty.

"His lungs, heart, and kidneys are all working well, thank God..." said Dr. Bryant.

"That's wonderful!" exclaimed Mrs. Bryant, never letting Dr. Sanders finish his sentence.

"Yes, yes, ma'am, but there is some bad news. In the

course of our evaluation, we found numerous spots all over his lungs, brain, and adrenal glands. I am pretty confident it is cancer that has widely spread all over his body."

Mrs. Bryant simply stared at Dr. Sanders, not believing what she has just heard.

"I am so..." began Dr. Sanders before he was interrupted.

"Dr. Sanders?" asked Mike the intern, looking down at the ground.

Dr. Sanders, frowning with disapproval, turned behind him and saw Mike, looking extremely frightened and nervous.

"I'm so sorry for disturbing you, sir, but I think you needed to see the cytology results on the CSF," said the intern, handing him the preliminary cytology report. This is the report of the analysis of the cells seen in the fluid surrounding Dr. Bryant's brain and spinal cord. When Dr. Sanders took the sheet, Mike quickly turned and left the room.

"Mike," said Dr. Sanders. Mike stopped dead in his tracks.

"I would like to speak with you after I finish with Mrs. Bryant," said Dr. Sanders. Mike froze with fear.

"Oh...OK, sir," said Mike. He walked out of the room in a cold sweat.

Dr. Sanders read the report, and it confirmed his suspicion:

MALIGNANT CELLS PRESENT. BASED ON CELLULAR CHARACTERISTICS AND PRELIMINARY STAINING, IT APPEARS TO BE AN ADENOCARCINOMA, LUNG PRIMARY FAVORED. FURTHER STAINING IS PENDING.

The lung cancer has even gotten into the fluid around the spinal cord.

"What is that?" asked Mrs. Bryant. She was barely able to speak.

"This is the cytology report on the CSF..." he realized that she will not understand what he just said.

Dr. Sanders was always conscious of the fact that patients and their families are not familiar with the medical jargon which doctors throw around. It can be frustrating when a doctor uses sophisticated medical terms with which a patient is not familiar, and Dr. Sanders was keenly aware of this.

"I'm sorry ma'am," chucked Dr. Sanders, "this is the report of the analysis of the cells in the fluid that bathes your husband's brain and spinal cord, the CSF. We found cancer cells in there, and they appear to come from the lungs. I am so sorry to tell that your husband has a very aggressive form of lung cancer."

"Cancer? How is this possible? He was as healthy as a horse!" said Mrs. Bryant angrily. "Are you sure you have the correct information? Are you sure you have not mixed up my Bill's records with someone else's?"

"I am quite sure, ma'am," said Dr. Sanders, "I double checked the information myself." Dr. Sanders did in fact double check the information (except for the cytology report) because, once, an intern gave him wrong information, and Dr. Sanders neglected to verify it. It almost led to a serious medical error. Now, he double checks everything.

"Well, can't it be treated? Cancer can be cured, can't it? I mean, this is Chicago Memorial Hospital. You have to be able to cure him here, of all places," said Mrs. Bryant.

"Well, ma'am, I am not sure his cancer is curable..." said Dr. Sanders, before being interrupted.

"But you are not a cancer specialist, Dr. Sanders. I want a cancer specialist to see my husband!" said Mrs. Bryant forcefully.

"Of course, of course, Mrs. Bryant. We have already called the cancer specialist to come and see your husband. But, again, I am not sure..."

"You are not a cancer specialist. I am sure he can find something to cure my husband with," said Mrs. Bryant.

"Let's just wait and see what she says, OK?" said Dr.

Sanders. He was trying really hard not to let his annoyance show through.

"Of course," said Mrs. Bryant, confident that her husband will be cured. "You need to cure my Bill, Dr. Sanders," said Mrs. Bryant. She began to cry as she continued, "He is all that I have left in this world that is worthwhile. I don't know what I would do without him..."

Dr. Sanders hugged Mrs. Bryant gently, "It's OK, Mrs. Bryant. It's OK. I know this is very hard for you. Rest assured that I am doing everything I can for your husband."

That remark gave Mrs. Bryant some desperately needed comfort. "Thank you, doctor," said Mrs. Bryant.

Dr. Sanders began to get up when he remembered one last thing, sitting back down in his chair.

"I almost forgot to ask you this ma'am. Did you and Dr. Bryant ever talk about end of life plans?"

Mrs. Bryant was taken aback by the question. "What do you mean," she asked incredulously.

"I mean, does your husband have a living will?" By the confused look on Mrs. Bryant's face, Dr. Sanders knew that she had no idea about what he was talking.

"Did Dr. Bryant ever address what he would want done to him in case of terminal illness..."

"My husband is not terminal!" exclaimed Mrs. Bryant.

"Ma'am, I'm sorry. I hate to bring this up, but it is important for me to know what Dr. Bryant would have wanted in case his heart stops."

"He would want everything done, of course!" said Mrs. Bryant, visibly angry.

"Are you sure that is what *he* wanted?" asked Dr. Sanders.

"You...do...everything...for...my...Bill.   You understand?" said Mrs. Bryant forcefully. She almost poked him in the chest.

"Yes, ma'am. Of course. I will do everything to save your husband," said Dr. Sanders, knowing full well that whatever he will do is ultimately futile. Yet, in the absence of any sort of direction from the patient, the patient's spouse becomes the medical decision maker. And she has made the decision to keep her husband alive at all costs.

Dr. Sanders got up to leave the room. "We will talk a little later. Why don't you go home and get some rest? I will definitely call you if anything comes up," said Dr. Sanders.

"My place is here, doctor. But, thank you," said Mrs. Bryant appreciatively. Her animosity at his asking her about end-of-life issues has vanished. That is how Mrs. Bryant dealt with difficult things: she would quickly empty them from her mind.

"Alright. Talk to you later, Mrs. Bryant," said Dr. Sanders, and he walked out of the room and turned to join the rest of the team, which was well on its way to finishing its morning rounds.

Almost as soon as Dr. Sanders left the room, in walked Susan Montgomery.

"Good morning, Mrs. Bryant" said Susan, with compassion in her voice and face. She walked over to her and rubbed her shoulders.

"You've been here all night? You poor thing!" she said.

"I can't bear to leave his side, Susan. What are you doing here?"

"I'm going to be your husband's nurse today!"

Mrs. Bryant smiled and said: "Well, isn't that nice."

11

"I hate hospitals," said Sarah as they approached the main entrance of Chicago Memorial Hospital. George was relieved that Sarah talked again. He pressed "END" on his cell phone once more.

"My God! I've called your mother several times, but she is not answering her phone."

"It's OK, George."

"I'm sure she will be thrilled to see you, my dear."

Sarah's experiences with hospitals were never pleasant. She has seen her share of hospitals since she ran away from home: it would usually start in the Emergency Room after a suicide attempt, and that would inevitably lead to a transfer to a psychiatric hospital. She would get some treatment, get better for a short while, and then relapse, leading her to try to take her life once again.

Sarah's vicious cycle of suicide attempt, hospitalization, discharge, and suicide attempt would have continued *ad nauseum* had it not been for her husband, who rescued her from the one time she would finally be successful.

"Here we are, my precious Sarah," said George. He pulled the car up to the main entrance and parked the car. He then got out and opened the door. Sarah, although hesitating at first, got out of the car.

"Thanks so much, George. It was so good to see you again," said Sarah, managing to eek out a smile to him.

George's eyes welled with tears once again.

"The pleasure was mine, my love," said George. "You have given me life once again. Ever since you left, I have been dying a slow death each and every day. The Lord brought you back to me, and I thank Him eternally for that."

Sarah reached up and gave George a big, long hug. George reached for her head and pushed it firmly into his chest, closing his eyes, which had tears streaming down them.

Sarah let go of George and turned toward the front door of the hospital. Just then, however, she froze. For reasons unknown, Sarah suddenly had cold feet, and she could not bring herself to walk through the front door. She stood there for what felt like an eternity. She had prepared for this moment for years. She went through this scenario in her mind a million times, yet when it finally faced her, she became scared. She wanted so badly to run back to her husband's arms in Seattle.

"Sarah?" asked George, putting his hand on her shoulder. "You alright, dear?"

His voice brought her back from her frozen trance.

"Yes, yes, I'm fine, George," said Sarah, reaching out and holding his hand. With that, she turned and walked inside the door. George stood there watching as she left him and disappeared into the revolving door. Even though Sarah was walking quickly toward the information desk, each step took a tremendous toll on her, nonetheless.

"Can I help you, ma'am?" asked the receptionist at the Information Desk.

"Yes, I'm here to see Dr. Bryant. I understand he's a patient here," said Sarah.

The receptionist looked up at Sarah for a moment.

"May I ask who you are?" asked the receptionist, a heavy-set woman in her 50s wearing reading glasses that are on the edge of her nose.

Sarah was even more surprised at the question. There were strict instructions not to let any visitors to see

Dr. Bryant. Mrs. Bryant wanted complete privacy.

"I'm...I'm his daughter." She barely could utter those words. She had been running away from that fact for so many years, and now that she had to face it head on, it was nearly unbearable. All she could think about was her husband.

The receptionist picked up the phone and dialed the extension to the ICU.

"Yes, this is Reception, and I have someone claiming to be Dr. Bryant's daughter wanting to see him," said the attendant, whose name was also Sarah.

"His daughter?" asked the ICU Unit Clerk in complete shock.

"That's what she says," replied Sarah the Reception attendant.

"Hmm...I'm going to have to clear this with his nurse and Mrs. Bryant."

"If you can have a seat, ma'am. The ICU will be right with you," said the receptionist to Sarah.

"Is there a problem?" asked Sarah, confused over the restriction.

"There are strict orders not to let in any visitors, ma'am."

"Even for his daughter?" asked Sarah with a

simultaneously confused and annoyed look.

"I'm sorry, ma'am, but that is what Mrs. Bryant wants."

Sarah heard that name, "Mrs. Bryant," and froze. All the memories of what had happened to her, and her mother's willing acquiescence, had slammed her all at once. It was too much to bear, and she ran out of the Hospital's front door, crying.

"Ma'am? Ma'am? Are you OK?" said the receptionist as Sarah ran outside.

Sarah stood outside for a long time crying and shaking, and the will to continue on with this mission was quickly fading. Meanwhile, the ICU unit clerk went up to Susan, who was attending to her lover in MICU-7.

"There is someone at the front of the hospital claiming to be Dr. Bryant's daughter and wanting to see him."

Susan was shocked.

"His daughter? Dr. Bryant doesn't have a daughter."

"That's what this person downstairs is saying."

"I have to ask Mrs. Bryant, but she has stepped out to get freshened up."

"I will let Reception know."

The clerk walked back to the ICU front desk and dialed the receptionist's extension.

"They have to clear it with Mrs. Bryant."

"The lady started crying and ran outside," said the receptionist.

"Wow. Well, maybe she wasn't who she said she was. Alright then. Thanks, dear."

"Have a good day."

Susan took advantage of the fact that no one was in the room besides she and her lover. She looked around to make sure no one was coming, and she closed the curtain at the door of the ICU room. She then went close to Dr. Bryant and kissed him gently on his forehead.

"I'm here, baby. I will take good care of you, my love. I…I love you so much…"

She started to tear up, but she quickly wiped her tears and tried to cover up any trace of her encounter with her lover. She opened up the curtain once again, so no one would suspect anything.

Meanwhile, Sarah was outside the front door of the hospital quietly sobbing. She so badly wanted to call a taxi and go back home to Seattle. But, there was something preventing her from doing so.

You can do this. You came all this way. You have to do this to move on, Sarah.

Suddenly, she felt a strength surge inside of her, which gave her the determination to continue. From where it came, she knew not, but it was strong nonetheless. So, she went back inside the hospital, but this time she avoided the front desk reception area and was able to enter into the hospital undetected.

"Excuse me," Sarah asked a hospital volunteer. "Do you know how I can get to the ICU?"

"Take Elevator F to the seventh floor. You can follow the signs to take you to Elevator F. It is a bit confusing, do you want me to take you there?" replied the volunteer, smiling widely.

"No, no, ma'am. Thank you, I can manage," said Sarah, wiping the last few tears to escape her eyes.

"Are you alright, dear?" asked the volunteer, whose smile turned into a look of concern. "Is someone you know sick?"

"My father is critically ill."

"Oh my God! I'm so sorry. I hope he gets better."

Smiling, Sarah said, "Thank you very much. Elevator F?"

"Yes, dear, to the seventh floor."

"Thank you."

Elevator F was a bit difficult to find, but Sarah was able to navigate around the very posh front lobby, past the upscale furniture and live plants that were strategically placed all across the lobby. She walked past the Starbucks counter and the Panera mini-store. There were people, attending doctors (wearing long blue lab coats), medical students (wearing short white lab coats), and residents (wearing long gray lab coats) walking in every direction. Some were walking briskly, some were walking slowly, and some were running. Many were sitting on the many chairs sipping Starbucks coffee and laughing with their colleagues.

After a few turns, she found Elevator F, and a door was already open, as if it was waiting for her to come in. When she went to press "7" on the panel, she was surprised to find it already pressed. Almost as soon as she pulled her finger away from the button labeled "7," the doors closed, and the elevator started going up. As the elevator quickly ascended, her stomach sank even more quickly. Before she could take another breath, the tone rang, and she was on the seventh floor.

The doors opened, and she looked at the sign directly in front of her directing people to the various wards on the seventh floor. It was quite simple: the MICU (medical intensive care unit) was to the right, and the CICU (cardiac intensive care unit) was to the left. Sarah turned right and a little down the hall was too frosted glass doors with the big letters "MICU" printed across them. They were locked, and a sign to her right directed her to pick up the phone and dial the numbers 4550, which would connect her to the main reception desk in the MICU. Sarah followed the instructions, and she heard the phone ringing.

"MICU, Ms. Johnson speaking," said the voice on the phone. That was the unit clerk in the MICU, Clara Johnson.

Sarah hesitated to speak.

"Hello?" said Ms. Johnson. Before she was going to hang up, Sarah spoke up.

"Yes, I am here to visit the patient in Bed 7," said Sarah, clearing her throat.

There was a long pause on the phone, and this time it was Sarah who chimed in.

"Hello?" said Sarah.

"Please, ma'am, come right in," said Ms. Johnson, and there was a metallic clang, indicating the lock on the door has been released. Sarah looked and found the large square metal push plate underneath the phone with the word "PUSH" imprinted on it. She pushed it, and the big glass doors opened up automatically. Sarah walked in, and the front reception was directly behind the doors. The ICU was vast, and it continued seemingly forever in front of her. There were people everywhere, and, as was said before, it was a very noisy place.

Ms. Johnson looked at Sarah with a stunned gaze, although she was trying (rather unsuccessfully) to mask her surprise.

"Can you tell me where Bed 7 is?" asked Sarah.

"May I ask who you are, ma'am?" said Ms. Johnson.

"I'm...I'm Sarah Bryant, Dr. Bryant's daughter."

Her eyes widened when she said those words, and she picked up the phone and dialed Susan's portable phone which she carried with her.

"Susan, honey, there is someone outside at the desk asking to see Dr. Bryant. Have you spoken to Mrs. Bryant?"

"Not yet. Who is it?"

"You said he is your father?" asked Ms. Johnson, totally surprised, turning to Sarah and holding the phone in her hand.

"Yes, is there a problem?" Sarah's annoyance began to grow exponentially.

"No, no problem, ma'am. It's just that Mrs. Bryant does not want any visitors. And we are unaware of any other children for Dr. Bryant besides Dr. Bob."

"Dr. Bob?" asked Sarah.

"Yes, Dr. Robert Bryant, his son. He is a Cardiac Surgeon at this hospital as well."

Sarah's eyes widened at this fact. She had no idea that her brother had followed in their father's footsteps.

During this time, Susan had come up to the front desk.

"Excuse me," said Susan, "I'm Susan Montgomery, Dr. Bryant's nurse. Can I help you, miss…"

"Sarah Mey…Sarah Bryant. Dr. Bryant's daughter."

"Dr. Bryant has no daughter, ma'am," said Susan defensively. She was sure she knew everything there is to know about her critically ill lover.

Sarah, shocked and angered at Susan's brazenness, said, "How dare you? I am Sarah Bryant, his daughter. I demand to see my father."

Shaking her head, Susan said, "I'm sorry, but Dr. Bryant is to have no visitors. Mrs. Bryant has given strict instructions…"

"Where is she? Can I speak to her, please?" asked Sarah angrily.

"I am right here," said Mrs. Bryant, startling the both of them and causing them to turn around to face her.

Both Sarah and Mrs. Bryant froze in total horror.

Sarah could not believe how much her mother had aged, and her mother looked as if she had seen a ghost, or someone raised from the dead. Sarah was raised from the dead, as far as her mother was concerned, because Sarah had died in her mother's eyes years ago. Yet, there was something, deep down in her heart, that always reassured her that Sarah was still alive, and this is why Mrs. Bryant immediately recognized that Sarah was indeed her long lost daughter.

After a long pause, it was Sarah who talked first: "Hello, mother." All those at the front desk gasped.

Mrs. Bryant, completely bewildered, nearly fell to the ground. Susan quickly rushed to her side, preventing her from falling completely to the floor.

"Mrs. Bryant! Are you OK?" asked a breathless Susan. She turned and looked at Sarah, who was still frozen in her place.

Gathering her strength, Mrs. Bryant slowly walked up to Sarah and looked straight into her eyes, standing no more than 12 inches away from her. She then reached for the top of her hair and felt it in her fingers. She then let out a shriek and threw herself into Sarah's arms.

"My Sarah, my Sarah. Oh my Sarah, my precious, precious Sarah," said Mrs. Bryant. She could not control her sobbing. Sarah was crying profusely as well. Mrs. Bryant buried her head into Sarah's chest, and she let out muffled screams of "Oh my Sarah, my Sarah, my Sarah" in between her loud sobs. Everyone around the front desk was crying, except for Susan. She had her hands around her mouth in total shock.

Mrs. Bryant then fell to Sarah's feet.

"Oh my Sarah, I'm so sorry! I'm so sorr..." and she sobbed and sobbed. Sarah reached down, wiping tears from her eyes and face, pulling up her mother. "It's over, mother. The demons are dead."

Mrs. Bryant's sobbing suddenly stopped, and she looked straight into Sarah's eyes once again. Mrs. Bryant knew exactly what those four words, "*The demons are dead*," meant. After a few moments, she buried her face into Sarah's chest once again, sobbing and letting out the same muffled screams of "my Sarah, my Sarah, my Sarah." They stood there in each other's arms for several minutes, embracing each other ever so firmly. More and more people gathered around them, and they were whispering to each other about who Sarah was. When they learned the truth and beheld the scene of mother and long-lost daughter embracing, they were in total shock.

Sarah and Mrs. Bryant were completely oblivious to the large group of people gathered around them. Sarah then pulled her mother's face from her chest, her shirt now wet with her mother's tears, and put it between her hands, wiping her mother's tears.

"I'm home, Mom. I'm home," said Sarah, and she embraced her mother again. Mrs. Bryant would have stayed in her daughter's embrace all day if she had not suddenly remembered her critically ill husband laying no so far from the spot of their sacred reunion.

She almost "jumped" out of Sarah's arms.

"Your father..." said Mrs. Bryant in between sighs, "your father is so sick. He's...he's got cancer, and it's all over his body...and he's...on a breathing..." and Mrs. Bryant pulled Sarah into MICU Bed 7. Sarah was trying to resist, but her mother's pull was very strong, strangely. Mrs. Bryant almost yanked Sarah into her father's room, and Sarah was shocked at seeing her father on the ventilator with all the tubes going into him, all those IV poles surrounding his bed like a police guard.

She walked slowly towards her father's bedside, walking past her mother, who stood behind her a little to Sarah's right. A large group of people gathered outside the room to witness Sarah's seeing her father for the first time in more than a decade. Susan, noticing this entourage, closed the curtain to give the Bryant family their well-deserved privacy. Some outside gasped in annoyance.

At his bedside now, Sarah stood there motionless for a long while. All the times she practiced this scenario, she envisioned her father to be alive and well. Never did she imagine seeing her father like this, and oddly, a sense of disappointment and anger set in. She wanted to look into her father's eyes when she finally faced him and held him accountable for what he had done to her. She wanted to see his shame and remorse. She wanted to see his response. Sadly, his illness robbed her of all of that, and it made her angry. She drew on that anger to give her the strength to do what she did next. Bending toward her father's ear, Sarah spoke to her father for the first time in decades.

"Daddy?" said Sarah in a little girl's voice. She was crying now. "Daddy?" she repeated.

Dr. Bryant, heretofore breathing with the machine and not fighting it, began to breathe more quickly, almost seeming to fight the ventilator. The machine began to alarm, and the monitor also began to alarm: his heart rhythm became dangerously unstable. Almost immediately, Susan pushed through the people gathered outside Dr. Bryant's room.

"V-tach!" she screamed. She ran over across the bed to the monitor which was affixed to the ceiling opposite Sarah and Mrs. Bryant. She pressed a button which turned on the blood pressure machine. It took about 30 seconds and the reading was very low: 65/32. It was previously normal: 138/64. Susan then screamed to the group of people: "Get the crash cart! Call Dr. Sanders!" She was becoming more and more frantic as the seconds progressed. Soon, both Dr. Sanders and the fellow, Dr. Ahmed, came into the room.

"What's wrong?" asked Dr. Sanders.

"He's in V-tach and BP's low," said Susan. She was obviously nervous as she walked back and forth around the bed getting things ready.

Dr. Sanders turned to Sarah and her mother, who were both crying now.

"What's wrong, doctor?" asked Sarah.

"He's having a dangerous heart rhythm and we need to work on him. Could you please step out? We will come get you as soon as we're done, OK?" Dr. Sanders said in as soothing a tone as possible.

Sarah and her mother left the room as more people entered it to help with the situation.

"Who's that woman with Mrs. Bryant?" asked a bewildered Dr. Sanders to Susan.

"His daughter!" replied an equally bewildered Susan.

Dr. Sander's eyes widened in shock. "His daughter?" Quickly, however, Dr. Sanders re-focused on the task at hand.

Just then, as Sarah and her mother were outside the room, Dr. Brian Frank walked into the ICU toward Dr. Bryant's room. Mrs. Bryant saw that she came and was relieved, grabbing on to her hand.

"Oh Brian! Brian, something's happened to Billy!" she said crying.

Surprised, Dr. Frank replied, "What's happened?"

"I don't know, something about his heart," said Mrs. Bryant. Just as she said that word, a frantic sounding alarm sounded and a red light began to flash just outside Dr. Bryant's room. Suddenly, an announcement blared over the PA system of the hospital.

"Code Blue MICU...Code Blue MICU...Code Blue MICU"

Dr. Frank went into the room to see what had happened, leaving Sarah and Mrs. Bryant outside in shock and horrific worry.

12

"Goddamit!" yelled Dr. Sanders. He was standing to the right of the bed, which was shaking violently from the chest compressions being delivered by John Thomas, one of the few male nurses working that day in the ICU, who came into the room as soon as the "CODE BLUE" was called. A number of other people had responded to the Code and are in the room as well.

Dr. Bryant's heart rhythm deteriorated even further, and he lost his pulse. It went from a fast heart beat to a flat line, called asystole. The room was packed with people, and there was barely enough room to stand. There was a respiratory therapist at the head of the bed with a bag pushing air into the breathing tube. During these "code" situations, the ventilator is almost always disconnected from the patient.

"Hold compressions, please," said Dr. Sanders. He said these words with almost ice cold calm, even though he let out occasional curses in frustration. He *never* panicked during a "CODE BLUE." In fact, at the beginning of each rotation, he would gather the ICU team and tell them this:

"The first five rules of any emergency situation in the ICU are these: 1. Don't panic. 2. Don't panic. 3. Don't panic. 4. Don't panic. 5. Don't panic."

"Still asystole. Continue CPR," said Dr. Sanders. "When was the last epi?" he asked. "Epi" stands for "epinephrine," which is adrenaline, given during cardiac arrest.

"Three minutes ago," said the charge nurse, who was also in the room and charting down the events on a form on a clipboard.

"Give another epi, please," said Dr. Sanders. The nurse then continued to give chest compressions.

"What happened?" asked Dr. Frank, who was watching unbeknownst to Dr. Sanders. His question startled him a bit. Susan was doing a very bad job at hiding her panic at the fact that Dr. Bryant's heart had stopped.

"Oh! Brian! Hey. I didn't see you...V-Tach turned into V-Fib," Dr. Sanders said, turning to face Dr. Frank.

"No problem Joe. Don't let me bother you."

"Thanks," said Dr. Sanders smiling and turning back

to the situation at hand.

"Great chest compressions, Mike. Just great," said Dr. Sanders.

Mike, who was sweating profusely from administrating the chest compressions, didn't reply, but appreciated the compliment. It kept him going. After about 1 minute, Dr. Sanders chimed in again:

"Hold compressions, please." He then looked at the monitor and the heart rhythm was a swiggly line, which is called "ventricular fibrillation."

"OK, give a shock," said Dr. Sanders. Susan, now profusely sweating, then pressed a button labeled "Charge" on a small monitor on the right side of Dr. Bryant's bed which was connected to two pads that are stuck to his chest. The monitor then emitted a sound with an increasing pitch, indicating that it was charging. When it was done charging, it emitted another sound.

"All clear!" yelled Susan. Immediately, everyone moved away from the bed, to avoid being shocked. Susan then pressed the button on the monitor machine, and Dr. Bryant jerked from the electricity that was just delivered to his body. A regular heart rhythm returned.

"OK," said Dr. Sanders. "Do we have a pulse?" he asked.

"Strong pulse," yelled Mike, who was feeling with his

finger on Dr. Bryant's neck, where one of the main arteries, the carotid artery, lies.

"All right, what's the BP?" asked Dr. Sanders.

Susan went over to the main monitor above Dr. Bryan't bed and pressed a button labeled "Start," which activates the machine which measures BP. After about 45 seconds, the monitor read 122/46.

"OK..." said Dr. Sanders.

"Nice job, Joe," said Dr. Frank smiling. Secretly, he wished his adversary had died, but he did a good job of hiding this feeling.

"Thanks," said Dr. Sanders, but he had no satisfaction on his face.

"But, it's not like I did him a favor. His brain is totally fried, and he has widely metastatic lung cancer. I tried to explain this to his wife, but she was hearing nothing of it. 'Do everything' she told me." Dr. Sanders put up his hands in frustration. Susan really resented that, and she scowled at Dr. Sanders, but he didn't see it.

"Ah, I see. Do you want me to talk to Mrs. Bryant?"

"Oh, no! Thanks, Brian. I will talk to her," said Dr. Sanders appreciatively. He reached out and patted him on the shoulder.

"Carry on here," said Dr. Frank, nodding to Dr.

Sanders and walking out of the room.

Sarah and Mrs. Bryant almost jumped at the site of Dr. Frank coming out of the room.

"Brian? How is he? What happened?" asked a frantic Mrs. Bryant.

"Well, his heart…I'm sorry," looking at Sarah, "Miss…" Dr. Frank didn't want to disclose medical information to an unauthorized person.

"Oh!" said Mrs. Bryant, "this is our daughter, Sarah."

Dr. Frank was clearly taken aback by this news, and he looked at Sarah with wide eyes.

"It's nice…nice to meet you," said Sarah, extending her hand to Dr. Frank.

"The pleasure is mine," said Dr. Frank, shaking her hand. He looked at Mrs. Bryant in total shock and said: "I didn't know you and Bill also had a daughter."

Mrs. Bryant paused a bit and Sarah chimed in, "We've been…estranged, but when my father became sick, I decided to come."

"Oh," said Dr. Frank with a sober look. "Well, I'm very sorry to meet you under *these* circumstances."

Sarah smiled slightly.

Just then, Dr. Sanders and Dr. Ahmed came out of

the ICU room with a number of other people. They walked straight to Sarah, Mrs. Bryant, and Dr. Frank. Mrs. Bryant looked straight at Dr. Sanders.

"How's my husband?"

"He's stable," sighed Dr. Sanders. "His heart developed a dangerous rhythm, but we were able to bring him back."

"Thank you very much, doctor," said Mrs. Bryant.

"My pleasure," said Dr. Sanders, lying through his teeth.

Dr. Sander's gaze went straight to Sarah.

"So, I hear Dr. Bryant also has a daughter?" he asked in total surprise.

"Yes," chimed in Mrs. Bryant. "This is Sarah, our daughter."

"Nice to meet you," said Dr. Sanders, extending his hand to Sarah.

"Nice to meet you," said Sarah, extending her hand and shaking his.

"Wow. Bobby's sister. I will have a few words with him next time I see him," said Dr. Sanders, trying to make a joke. No one was laughing.

Dr. Sanders coughed embarrassedly and tried to

quickly change the subject.

"Um...you can go in to see your husband now, Mrs. Bryant," said Dr. Sanders with a straight face.

"Thank you, doctor."

Dr. Sanders quickly walked away and sat down in front of a computer.

Mrs. Bryant and Sarah then walked into the ICU room, where Susan was frantically working to fix everything up after the CODE BLUE.

"Hello there," said Susan turning to Mrs. Bryant and Sarah. "We had a close call, but Dr. Bryant is OK."

"Thank God," said Mrs. Bryant.

"Please, have a seat." Susan pulled up two chairs to the bedside for them to sit.

They both smiled at Susan and sat down next to Dr. Bryant.

"Susan," said Dr. Frank peeking in through the door of the room, "may I speak with you for a moment?" He smiled at the Bryants, who smiled back.

"Sure, Dr. Frank," said Susan cheerfully as she walked out of the room. Dr. Frank led her to a less populated hall just off the main ICU area.

The smile on his face just a few seconds ago was long

gone, replaced by a stern scowl.

"This is *highly* inappropriate."

Susan, shocked, replied: "What is highly inappropriate?"

Scoffing, Dr. Frank said, "Really?"

"Dr. Frank, I don't understand," said Susan with a look of total confusion (she was telling the truth at that moment, actually).

"You don't think that the fact that Dr. Bryant's *mistress* is assigned to be his nurse is at all inappropriate? At all?"

Susan stood there completely speechless.

"With his *wife* and *daughter...at the bedside?*" he said pointing to the room. He was incredulous that she didn't know to what he was referring.

Susan had no response, looking at him with wide eyes of shock.

Pointing right at her face, "Get off his case...NOW." He then turned and walked briskly out of the ICU, leaving Susan standing frozen with fear and embarrassment.

She slowly walked to the Charge Nurse, Tanya, trembling. She thought the secret of their affair was well-kept. She knew now, to her horror, that she was wrong.

"What's wrong?" asked Tanya, eyes full of concern.

"I...I need to be reassigned off of Dr. Bryant's case."

"Why? Is there a problem?" asked Tanya with surprise.

"I...I have an emergency at home and have to leave."

"Oh my God! Is everything OK? Can I help with something," said Tanya with even more concern now.

"No, no. I'm...I'm fine," said Susan, tearing up. Tanya reached out and hugged Susan.

"Thank you," said Susan, sniffing and wiping her tears.

Susan walked back to the ICU room, and Tanya walked behind her worried about her friend and colleague.

"Why, Susan? What ever is the matter dear?" asked a concerned Mrs. Bryant.

"I...I apologize, but I must leave to tend to an emergency at home," said Susan, wiping away tears.

"Oh my God! Is everything OK?" asked Mrs. Bryant.

"I hope so, ma'am. Another nurse will take my place in short order," said Susan, crying and looking away from her and Sarah. She actually could not look at either of them.

"Well, take care, my dear. Please let us know if we can do anything at all," said Mrs. Bryant, with a look of sympathy.

Susan acknowledged her kindness with a nod, and walked out of the room.

"What a nice person," said Mrs. Bryant, and Sarah nodded in agreement.

They then both returned to tending to Dr. Bryant, who was dying of metastatic cancer. The tragedy was, neither of them realized this at the time.

"My God! Bobby!" gasped Mrs. Bryant. "I have to call him! He doesn't know you've come home!"

Mrs. Bryant looked at Sarah with a smile, and she pulled out her cell phone and dialed Dr. Bob's cell phone number. She tried several times, but his voicemail kept picking up.

"I wonder why he's not picking up his phone," asked Mrs. Bryant, with a look of confusion and concern. Sarah, for her part, was nervous as she dialed his number. She didn't know what to expect. In fact, she as bit relieved he didn't answer.

"I hope nothing is wrong..."

13

The silence and darkness of the room was both deafening and blinding. As his breathing slowed to a deathly pace, the nightmares and flashes of the past accelerated in his mind. In succeeding fashion, ugly memories of a brutal father subjecting this once sensitive, mild-mannered boy to a brutal childhood. First, it was sexual abuse: something he thought a father normally did to his young son, until his sister came of age. He then changed the abuse from sexual to physical.

That is not to mention the taunts, the mocking, the harassment, and the imposition of the father's will on the son. Over time, this sensitive, sweet boy became hardened and bitter; perpetually angry; continually frustrated. That anger turned into hateful rage, which at once destroyed him yet, strangely, also motivated him to succeed. Yet, all that began to unravel as of late, and his life began to crumble around him.

Part of him wanted to give up, to slip away into the dark nothingness into which he was falling. Part of him wanted to rest, to escape from the daily pain, suffering, and torture to which this worldly life subjected him. Yet, there was another part that could not let go, that wanted yet to accomplish something, and that part's stamina was extremely strong. It pulled him out of the dark nothingness and into the light.

He then gasped out of the light back into darkness, but this time, it was the darkness of the call room in which he was sleeping. He woke up with a pounding headache, and the room was spinning around him. He was in a cold sweat, and he was trembling almost uncontrollably. He got up out of bed and proceeded to collapse to the floor. There he laid for several minutes, and then he slowly got up. His cell phone rang multiple times, but he didn't have the energy to even look at its direction. It felt as if his arms and legs were made of bags of sand, and it was a very difficult task to walk to the bathroom and turn on the light.

When he looked into the mirror, he was horrified by what he saw: a near skeleton of a man, the consumed shell of a once mild-mannered, sensitive boy who was chewed up and spit out. His head was still pounding, and when the realization of it all came crashing down, he fell to the ground sobbing uncontrollably. The tears streamed down his face and dripped onto the floor, because he was lying prostrate on the floor, as a Muslim prays toward Mecca five times a day. Yet, he was not singing praises to Allah. He was yelling curses out to the bathroom floor.

He cried so much that he threw up; no food came out, as he had not eaten in days. Rather, the acidic secretions of a stomach deprived of food came spewing out, burning all the tissue on its way out of his body. Then, seemingly out of nowhere, his crying stopped. The dejected sadness he felt was slowly transforming, transforming into ravenous rage. The rage seemed to well up from his feet and explode into his head. It moved him to stand up, dry his tears, and take another hard look at himself in the mirror. He hated what he saw, so much so, that he punched the mirror several times, bloodying his hand in the process. Awakened out of his rage by the pain of the shards of glass that cut his hand, he looked down at his hand and saw the blood streaming down onto the floor, covering the vomit that laid beneath him.

He grabbed a towel that was hanging to his right and wrapped his right hand to try to stop the bleeding. He then turned off the light in the bathroom and left the call room, with the light from the hallway briefly illuminating the cramped, dark room that the hospital designers believed would be sufficient to give rest and relaxation to overworked physicians. His arms and legs still felt like sand bags, but the rage he felt gave him an unusual strength. He was determined to do something, but he was not sure what that was. All that he knew now was that he had to go to the Emergency Department...to get his hand fixed.

He turned out of the call room and made a right, walking slowly down the hallway in a daze, squinting from the bright light of the hallway. In addition, bright sunshine was beaming from various patient rooms onto the floor. He found the elevator and took it to the bottom floor, where the Emergency Department was. He talked to one of the doctors on duty and asked him to take a look at his hand. He lied and said he slipped and fell on an examination table, and the ED physician knew it. Yet, judging by the way Dr. Bob looked, he decided not to delve into the situation. While he was being attended to in the ED, he heard overhead, "Code Blue ICU" being repeated three times.

14

Sarah and Mrs. Bryant were standing back from the bed, horrified at the screaming alarm on the bed monitor. Several nurses rushed into the room, looking a little frantic. Dr. Bryant's heart went back into a dangerously unstable rhythm.

"Dr. Sanders!" screamed Jennifer, the new nurse assigned to take care of Dr. Bryant that day.

Soon, Dr. Sanders, along with the fellow and other team members, came back into the room. Although he tried to hide it, Dr. Sanders had a look of frustrated fatigue, as if he was saying, "Not again!" Another nurse moved to start CPR, and Dr. Sanders interjected.

"Wait," he said. "Let me try something." Dr. Sanders then moved to the side of the bed and forcefully punched Dr. Bryant's chest once with the flat part of his clenched fist. Everyone looked at Dr. Sanders with horror, family and staff alike. After he did that, his heart rhythm suddenly returned to normal. Everyone was shocked.

Dr. Sanders looked around to everyone's befuddled faces and said, "What? You guys have never heard of the precordial thump?"

The "precordial thump" is a forceful punch on the chest of a patient whose heart has gone into a specific type of dangerous rhythm. Sometimes, it can work to "stun" the heart back into the beating normally. It does the same job as electric shock, without the electricity. Most of the time it does not work; this time it did, and it made Dr. Sanders look like a genius.

"Alright, everybody, back to work," said Dr. Sanders, with deep-seated satisfaction.

Mrs. Bryant looked at Dr. Sanders with a look of extreme satisfaction; she was quite impressed. Even Sarah was taken aback by what she just saw, and it is typically quite hard to impress Sarah, given all that she has been through.

"I was lucky it worked this time," said Dr. Sanders to Sarah and her mother. He was trying to be humble, but the quiet satisfaction of knowing that he looked great beamed through quite clearly.

"Do you have any other questions?" asked Dr. Sanders.

"Yeah," said Sarah. "Why does his heart keep doing

this?"

"Well," said Dr. Sanders, "he is quite sick. His shock, along with the cancer, along with the multiple seizures have really taken a toll on his heart, and it keeps trying to stop. And we keep preventing that from happening." He wanted to say, "Eventually it is not going to work," but he held his tongue.

"And you keep on doing that, doctor," said Mrs. Bryant forcefully. "You keep on doing that."

"Yes, ma'am," said Dr. Sanders.

"By the way, doctor. When is the cancer specialist going to come?" asked Mrs. Bryant.

Just as Dr. Sanders was about to answer, a voice rang out from behind them:

"Right now," said the voice.

They all turned around to see Dr. Janet Davis, the head of oncology at Chicago Memorial Hospital.

"Dr. Davis!" exclaimed Dr. Sanders. "How are you?"

"Hello, Janet!" said Mrs. Bryant, and she walked over to her to kiss and embrace.

"Annie...I'm so, so sorry to have to see you under these circumstances," said Dr. Davis, with a look of sadness and pity.

"Thank you," said Mrs. Bryant, with sadness welling up over her.

"Dr. Sanders," said Dr. Davis, nodding in acknowledgment of his salutation. "It's nice to see you."

"Janet, this is our daughter Sarah," said Mrs. Bryant. She never got tired of saying that.

Dr. Davis' eyes widened in complete surprise, which she quickly composed and replied: "Pleasure to meet you."

"The pleasure is mine," said Sarah.

"Annie, do you mind if I examine Bill?" asked Dr. Davis.

"Please," said Mrs. Bryant, getting out of the way to allow Dr. Davis to move to the side of the bed. Dr. Davis then conducted a thorough examination of Dr. Bryant Jr., from head to toe. After putting her stethoscope back in her lab coat pocket, she turned to Mrs. Bryant and Sarah with a serious look on her face.

"Annie," said Dr. Davis. "I have taken a look at Bill's scans, records, and lab results, including the cytology from the CSF."

"Uh...that is the fluid bathing his brain and spinal cord, remember," interjected Dr. Sanders, who stayed to listen to what she had to say.

"Yes," said Dr. Davis quickly, a little annoyed at the interjection by a quite junior faculty member.

She then turned to Mrs. Bryant and Sarah with a look of extreme pain.

"I…I don't know how to say this, but I am afraid that there is nothing we can to do about Bills' illness. The cancer has spread all over his body, and given his critical condition, giving chemotherapy will offer no benefit. In fact, it will do the opposite."

"What do you mean," asked Mrs. Bryant, quite confused.

"The drugs used to treat cancers such as that Bill has," said Dr. Davis, "are quite toxic, and they will only cause more harm and side effects with minimal to no benefit."

"Annie…I think Bill has terminal cancer."

Mrs. Bryant stood there frozen in shock.

"I'm so, so sorry."

Mrs. Bryant started sobbing into Sarah's shoulder, and Dr. Davis reached out to put her hand on her shoulder, but Mrs. Bryant moved away in anger. Dr. Davis winced in pity at the grief of her friend.

Sarah, holding her mother in her arms, asked: "Is there truly nothing you can do? No treatment that can be given? Nothing at all? With all the marvels of modern medicine, nothing can be offered to my father, the head of heart surgery?"

"I'm so sorry," sighed Dr. Davis. "If there was anything I could do, I would do it in a heartbeat. Your father was...is a dear colleague. If there was anything I could do for him, I would not hesitate," said Dr. Davis, upset for her Freudian slip. That statement, however, was a bald-faced lie. She hated Dr. Bryant.

She always thought him to be an arrogant, abrasive asshole. She once told him that to his face. "You just want me in bed," he retorted, and this enraged her further. She turned away and said under her breath, "Asshole." In fact, she often wondered why Mrs. Bryant could stand living in the same house as he, but she never dared bring this up to her. Despite Dr. Davis' hatred for her husband, she and Mrs. Bryant have always been good friends.

Many of the medical staff members felt the same way about Dr. Bryant as Dr. Davis. Some people can get to where Dr. Bryant. was by being polite, helpful, and accommodating. Dr. Bryant, on the other hand, got to where he was by being harsh and hard-hearted. And now that he is in dire need, there is no one who is able or willing to come to his aid, because all the bridges to him have long been burnt to ashes.

"I know this is very difficult news to take, Annie," said Dr. Davis to a still crying Mrs. Bryant. "But, at this point, as a friend and not an Oncologist, I would make Bill comfortable."

Sarah, still comforting her sobbing mother, widened her eyes at those words. She was surprised at their bluntness.

"I am truly sorry. Annie, I'm here if you need anything. And it was very nice to meet you," said Dr. Davis, putting her hand on Sarah's arm.

"Thank you, Doctor."

Dr. Davis then walked out of the room, and Dr. Sanders, who heretofore had been quiet, now spoke up.

"Was that all clear to you, Mrs. Bryant? Do you understand what is going on in your husband?" asked Dr. Sanders.

"Perfectly clear. You are abandoning my husband," said Mrs. Bryant, looking up from Sarah's shoulder, her face drenched with tears.

"No, no, no, ma'am. We are not doing that," said Dr. Sanders, with a look of disappointment.

"Mrs. Bryant," said Dr. Sanders, "rest assured we are doing everything we can for your husband. But, unfortunately, he has a very bad disease. Lung cancer is the most deadly cancer, and the type your husband had is quite aggressive and ultimately fatal. There is really nothing more we can do. So, the choice we have before us, and it is a terrible one to make, is to either continue aggressive care, which will only prolong his suffering and prolong the dying process, or make him comfortable and let him die naturally." Dr. Sanders was trying to be polite and nice, but it was becoming much more difficult.

"You are going to let my husband die?" asked Mrs. Bryant in horror. "What sort of doctor are you? Are you even a doctor?"

"Mom!" exclaimed Sarah.

Dr. Sanders looked at Sarah with understanding.

"It's OK. I understand you are frustrated," he said. "But I have to be absolutely truthful with you. Your husband is going to die from this disease, sooner or later. And what we are doing is only prolonging the dying process. I really do not think there is any hope for a meaningful recovery. That is why I broached the subject of end-of-life issues. If this were my father…"

"Well, he is *not* your father, Dr. Sanders," interrupted Mrs. Bryant loudly. "He is my husband, and you will do everything for him, do you understand? Everything!"

"Yes, ma'am, I understand. We are doing everything for your husband. I will come back later. Take care, ma'am," said Dr. Sanders, and with that, he walked out of the room.

Sobbing, Mrs. Bryant said, "I need some air. I need to get outside. Take me outside, Sarah. Give me some air."

"Yes mother," said Sarah. "Let's go get some coffee." She and her mother then went into the elevator and went downstairs to the lobby. They bought two cups of coffee and walked outside to get some air.

As they were leaving, Susan Montgomery was in the bathroom that was outside of the ICU. She was sobbing uncontrollably and throwing up at the same time.

15

"I hope that is not your Dad," said Dr. Thomas, one of the attending physicians in the Emergency Department who was cleaning Dr. Bob's wounds on this hand.

"My Dad?" said Dr. Bryant, shocked at his statement. Dr. Thomas, who along with everyone else knew about his father's medical illness, was surprised at Dr. Bob's question.

"You don't know?"

"Know what?"

"Your Dad is in ICU, intubated. I heard he is pretty bad."

"What?"

Dr. Bob looked as if he had seen a ghost.

"We may need a few sutures here," said Dr. Thomas, pointing to the irregular gash on his hand which he punched into the mirror only a few minutes earlier.

"Is that OK? Do you want Plastics to come see you?"

Dr. Bob did not answer.

"Dr. Bryant?" asked Dr. Thomas, surprised. "Should I call Plastics?"

"Huh..." gasped Dr. Bob, "...uh...no,no. Just take care of it, ok?" He was a bit annoyed that his train of thought was disturbed.

"Alright, alright," trying to comfort him. He reached over and picked up a package of sterile gloves. He opened the package and put the gloves on his hands. Then, keeping his hands in the air in front of him, so as not to contaminate them by touching anything, Dr. Thomas walked stepped out of the room slightly and yelled out for the nurse to come help him, as he now has lost his ability to touch anything that is not sterile.

"Angela!" he said loudly, but gently.

"Yeah?" could be heard from a distance.

"Could you come and help me suture bed 7, please?" asked Dr. Thomas.

"Will be right there Dr. Thomas, " said Angela Perkins, a young and relatively new nurse working in the ED.

Angela walked into the room and with a smile on her face said, "Hi Dr. Bryant! I am sorry about what happened to your hand...and your Dad."

Dr. Bryant did not answer, and this quickly erased her happy demeanor.

"Angela," said Dr. Thomas, trying to diffuse the tension of the moment, "can you hold up the lidocaine for me?"

"Sure, Dr. Thomas," Angela said, and she lifted up a vial labeled "Lidocaine 2%," which is medication to numb the skin so that the suture needle does not hurt. She held it upside down, with the cap facing down. Dr. Thomas then took a syringe with a needle on the end of it and put it into the cap. Once the needle was in the vial, he squirted some air into the bottle and then drew out most of the clear liquid that was in the vial.

Dr. Thomas then squirted and tapped the syringe so that all the air was removed. As he moved closer to Dr. Bryant's hand, Dr. Bryant began to pay more attention to what Dr. Thomas was doing.

"This is going to sting…"

He injected the Lidocaine and Dr. Bob winced in significant pain, and his hand began to shake a little.

"It's OK," said Dr. Thomas reassuringly.

After making several injections, the area around Dr. Bob's gash was totally numb, and he relaxed significantly.

Dr. Thomas began placing several sutures in his hand laceration, with Angela assisting him.

"So…my Dad is in ICU?"

"Yeah, I'm really surprised that you don't know."

"I've…I've been sick," he said, sniffing briefly.

"I'm real sorry about your Dad, man."

"Thanks," said Dr. Bob, looking out into space. He didn't know what to do with this new information.

It didn't take very long for Dr. Thomas to finish up suturing Dr. Bob's hand. After he finished, he bandaged up his hand.

"Get a wound check in three days, and you can come back in seven days to get the sutures out. Or…you can take them out yourself if you want," said Dr. Thomas smiling.

Dr. Bob didn't answer, and Dr. Thomas' smile went away.

Dr. Bob got up to leave as Angela was cleaning up the supplies.

"Be careful, OK?"

"Thanks," said Dr. Bob, already half way out of the room.

"I hope he is OK," said Dr. Thomas to Angela.

"Yeah, he looks terrible."

16

"Do you feel a little better, now?"

The air was already beginning to get quite warm, and the breeze was refreshing and invigorating. The sun was well into the sky, but not yet at the zenith. The city was bustling with activity, and cars were whizzing past in each direction. Car horns could be heard in the distance as Sarah and Mrs. Bryant were walking, arm in arm, next to Chicago Memorial Hospital. They were both holding cups of coffee as well, and Sarah kept rubbing her mother's shoulder.

"Yes, Sarah, I feel better," said Mrs. Bryant, still shocked at what had just transpired not too long before.

"I can't believe it. I just can't believe it. I can't believe that they said he is dying. I can't believe that they can do nothing for him," said Mrs. Bryant. "I can't believe he could do something like that to me. After all the years I gave him, I can't believe he would do something like that, Sarah."

"Mother, it's not like he meant to get sick."

"But," she said while she started crying, "he said he would always be there for me...he said that he would always..."

She couldn't control her crying, and Sarah did her best to comfort her mother.

Sarah remained silent for several moments, reflecting over her mother's grief at her father's illness. She had a range of emotions: sadness at her mother's grief, happiness that she is reunited with her mother, anger at her mother's complete oblivion of what had happened to her, why she left all those years ago.

She was going to continue to remain silent, but decided against it. *If I don't say it now, I am never going to say it again. This is why I came here in the first place.*

"Mother," Sarah said calmly, "why?"

Mrs. Bryant stopped walking and turned to Sarah.

"What? What do you mean?" asked an incredulous Mrs. Bryant.

Sarah started crying.

"Why, Mother? Why?"

Sarah could not believe that her mother did not know what she was talking about. Anger began to well up inside. All this time, all this distance, all this trouble to get here, and her mother still seemed to be in terrible denial.

"Mother!" yipped Sarah. "You honestly have no idea what I am talking about?"

Sarah, tears streaming down her face, looked straight into her mother's eyes, and her mother felt them pierce her soul. She dropped her cup of coffee, splashing on the ground beneath them, splattering all over the pavement. Sarah jumped slightly back to avoid getting hit with hot cafe mocha.

"Why did you do nothing?" asked Sarah, again, looking straight into her mother's eyes with a look of intense pain and betrayal.

Mrs. Bryant started to sob, and she buried her face into Sarah's shoulder. Sarah stroked her hand over the back of her mother's head, and they both stood there in a long embrace.

"It's OK, Mama, it's OK. I have forgiven you, Mama. I have forgiven you," said Sarah.

"I'm so sorry, my baby. I'm so sorry..." sobbed Mrs. Bryant. That is all she could say.

"Shh, shh. It's all right, Mama. Everything is all right," said Sarah in a soothing, motherly voice. She looked and found a bench not too far from where they were

129

standing, and she led her mother to there, and then they both sat down. She then wiped the tears off her mother's face and smiled right into it. It warmed Mrs. Bryant's heart to the core.

There was a long silence, with Mrs. Bryant holding her daughter's hand and looking down at them. She then said, in a barely audible voice: "I tried…"

"What?"

"I tried…" said Mrs. Bryant, looking out into space now, but clearing her throat.

"I tried to stop him…but he nearly killed me."

Sarah looked at her mother in total shock.

"Mom, what do you mean?"

"I tried to stop him…I even picked up the phone to call the police. But…"

Mrs. Bryant could barely continue.

"But…he took the phone away from me and threw me on the ground. He kicked, and kicked, and kicked, and…the next thing I remember I was coughing up blood on our bed."

Sarah couldn't speak. Mrs. Bryant's face went blank as she told her this.

"He almost killed me, and every time I would even

look at him with disapproval, he would beat me."

Sarah started to cry, and she saw her mother in a completely new light.

"I actually wanted to go with you...but..."

She could barely continue through her tears

"I was too much of a coward...I'm so sorry, baby. I'm so..."

Mrs. Bryant buried her face into Sarah's shoulder, sobbing. She then lifted her face up and looked at Sarah.

"When you didn't come back, I formally buried you in my mind, but...something deep down never gave up hope that you were OK. And I can't tell you how happy that you have come back to me, my Sarah."

Mrs. Bryant held her face with both her hands, rubbing her cheeks and wiping away the tears streaming down Sarah's face.

Sarah felt that she owed her mother an explanation, especially since she now knows that her mother was not a willing accomplice to her father's crimes.

"I had to get away from Dad. I had to get away from you. I had to get away from everything," said Sarah, looking out into space, but then turning to focus on her mother.

"I ran, and ran, and ran. I ran as far away as I could, and my running took me to Seattle," Sarah said.

"Seattle?" gasped her mother.

"Yes," said Sarah. "So many terrible things happened to me over these years. So many terrible things, Mama," said Sarah. She was fighting the tears, her voice choking up with emotion.

"So many times, Mama, I cursed your name, but at the same time, I needed you to be with me," said Sarah.

"I'm so sorry, Sarah..."

Sarah reached and held her mother's hand, reassuring her.

"Yet," she continued, "if it wasn't for those terrible things, I would never have met Jonathan."

"Jonathan?" asked Mrs. Bryant.

"Yes," said Sarah smiling. "Jonathan Myers. He was a counselor at a shelter I was staying at, and he helped me recover from all my pain. We eventually got married," said Sarah, showing her mother her wedding ring. Mrs. Bryant was shocked to see it, even though it was obvious.

"Oh my precious Lord, Sarah, that's wonderful!" exclaimed Mrs. Bryant, and she gave her daughter a hug. Sarah hugged her mother back so hard; for so long she wanted a hug from her mother on the occasion of her wedding. Just then, Sarah's cell phone rang.

She reached into her purse and looked at the caller ID: it was Jonathan.

She opened the cell phone and said, "Hello?"

Sarah started crying as she was talking, "Yes, baby, I'm OK. I'm here with my mother at the hospital. My Dad is very sick."

She could not stop the emotion and tears from flowing. Although she conducted herself strongly on the outside, on the inside, she was the vulnerable, abused 15 year old daughter who left Chicago many years ago. Hearing Jonathan's voice was so soothing, so familiar. Even though she grew up here, Chicago became almost a foreign country to her.

Jonathan tried to soothe his wife as best as he could, realizing the limitations of his being thousands of miles away. He really wanted to be there.

"They're saying he has cancer that has spread all over his body. He is on a respirator, and he is in critical condition. I'm OK, but I so wish you were here, baby," said Sarah, continuing to cry. Jonathan continued to console his wife.

"Oh, Jonathan, wait, I want you to say hello to my mother," said Sarah, wiping tears from her eyes, and sniffing them from her nose. She handed the cell phone to her mother.

"Hello?" said Mrs. Bryant, a little hesitantly.

"Hello, Jonathan. It is so nice to meet you, son" said Mrs. Bryant. "I can't wait to meet you in person, dear." At that moment, Mrs. Bryant became motherly again; the roles were oddly reversed: Sarah the vulnerable daughter, and Mrs. Bryant the consoling mother.

"You take care, now, OK? Bye, bye. Here's Sarah." She handed the cell phone back to Sarah.

"Hello? Yeah, baby, I'm OK. I'm OK. I will call you later. I love you," said Sarah, and she closed the phone. And just like that, the roles have re-reversed.

"He sounds like a wonderful man," said Mrs. Bryant.

"He is, Mama, he is. I can't wait for you to meet him in person," said Sarah, and he face turned sad after she was able to eek out a smile. She thought of her father, who was lying in the ICU in critical condition.

"I wonder how Dad is doing," said Sarah.

"We'd better go back and see if anything else has come up," said Mrs. Bryant. Sarah nodded, and they both got up to go back to the ICU. They walked past the spilled cup of coffee, and Mrs. Bryant felt embarrassed.

"I'm sorry about the coffee, my dear," said Mrs.

Bryant.

"No worries, Mother. No worries," said Sarah, squeezing her mother's shoulders in her arms as they walked back to the Medical Intensive Care Unit.

17

"I *really* need to pee," said Jennifer. "Can you watch Bed 7 for me real quick?"

"No problem Jen," said Denise, her co-worker, with a smile, who needed to cover Jennifer's VIP patient in her absence.

No doubt, it was going to be a short absence, but no ICU nurse could just leave the ICU without letting someone know where they are, in case something bad happened. And in the ICU, bad things can happen at the drop of a dime. One of the most predictable aspects of Critical Care Medicine is that it is wholly unpredictable.

After talking to Denise, she turned to the exit doors of the ICU and pressed a push plate on the wall to her right to operate the large mechanical doors. The women's bathroom was not that far away from those doors on the right. There was a staff bathroom inside the ICU, but it was occupied, and Sarah *really* needed to go to the washroom. The two large doors opened with a mechanical hum, and she walked straight to the bathroom, rather hurriedly. She was in such a hurry that she did not notice Dr. Bob walking into the ICU and straight to his father's room. In fact, no one noticed that he walked into the ICU, and he was able to go right in undetected.

As soon as he walked in, he paused briefly in surprise at how his father looked: comatose; tubes coming in and out of him in multiple places; the ventilator quietly breathing for him; a forest of IV poles with numerous bags of life-saving and life-sustaining medications all around his bed. His surprise, however, quickly turned into angry indignation. He walked right up to his father and whispered in his ear.

"Does it hurt?...Are you in pain?"

His anger continued to increase with every sentence.

"Are you suffering, you piece of shit? Are you going through hell?...Like the hell you put me through?...Like the hel..."

He could barely continue, with tears of rage and deep sorrow streaming down his face.

"Like...like the hell you put Sarah through, you unbelievable bastard?"

He then stood up, reached over and turned off the alarms on the ventilator. He looked around to make sure no one could see him, and he disconnected his father from the ventilator. Dr. Bryant began to breathe much more heavily, seeing that now he has no help from the machine. His son then bent down and whispered once again in his father's ear.

"I hope you suffocate, you piece of rotten shit. I hope you suffer...I hope you...you DIE you..."

His fury at his father was interrupted by the oxygen level monitor that began beeping loudly. The ventilator, although silenced, had multiple red windows flashing, indicating that it had been disconnected. The alarm jarred him out of his rage, and he didn't want anyone to suspect that he was trying to kill his father, and so he reconnected the vent moments before Jennifer came running into the room in sheer panic.

"Oh!" she said, with complete relief on her face, "Dr. Bob! You're here." Jennifer was taken aback at his disheveled appearance.

"Uh...yes...yes, I am," said Dr. Bob, trying to look at the monitor and acting like he cared one iota about his father. "His sats went down for a bit, but he is OK now. It was transient."

"Oh, good. I was afraid he was going to code again."

"He has coded already?"

"Oh, you didn't know?" Jennifer was a little surprised at the fact that he didn't know what had happened with his father heretofore.

"No."

"Yeah, he coded a couple of times already. He is maxed on all pressors, and his pressure, as you can see," she said looking up at the monitor, "is barely in the 80s."

"Wow," said Dr. Bob with no emotion on his face.

"Oh my God!" blurted Mrs. Bryant, who came into the room with Sarah unbeknownst to both Dr. Bob and Jennifer. They both turned around to face them, startled at her outburst.

"Bobby! What's happened to you?" said Mrs. Bryant in total shock at the appearance of her son.

Dr. Bob didn't say anything. He looked at Sarah with a confused look on his face, as if she was someone who looked familiar but still unknown to him.

Mrs. Bryant walked up to her son and rubbed his face.

"Son," she said in total concern, "are you OK? Have you been sick?"

Dr. Bob backed away from his mother in annoyance, looking away from her. Mrs. Bryant was further shocked.

"What's wrong with you? Don't you recognize your

sister when you see her?"

Jennifer's eyes widened at those words, and she quickly became uncomfortable and walked out of the room. Sarah stood frozen in shock. Dr. Bob's eyes also widened in total shock, looking at Sarah intently.

"Hey...hey Bobby," said Sarah with a little fear in her voice.

Dr. Bob's didn't say anything at first, looking at Sarah intently.

"Bobby?" Sarah repeated.

"Don't...call...me...Bobby!" he said in quiet rage. "You have no right to say ANYTHING to me!" He cursed his sister, and at this curse, Sarah and Mrs. Bryant were shocked, and they both started to cry.

"Robert!" said Mrs. Bryant. "How dare you speak like that to your sister. She has come back to us...from the dead!"

These words brought out even more rage from Dr. Bob.

"She is still DEAD to me..." he says to his mother, with eyes of rage.

"You hear that? You are DEAD to me...DEAD!" he turns to his sister. His teeth are clenched as he spoke those words, but at the same time, tears are streaming down his face. Sarah's cries become more intense, and he turns and leaves the room, sniffing and wiping his nose.

"My precious Sarah! I'm so sorry, baby," said Mrs. Bryant, walking over and hugging her daughter. This time, Sarah buried her face into her mother's arms.

"I don't know what has gotten into him. I thought he would be so happy to see you. He was *devastated* when you left…"

Sarah had a twinge of guilt when she heard her mother say that, but then it quickly went away and was replaced by anger.

"It's OK, Mom," said Sarah, hugging her mother intently. As they were hugging, Susan re-entered the room.

"Susan!" exclaimed Mrs. Bryant with a smile. "You came back! Is your emergency over with?"

Barely being able to smile, Susan said sheepishly, "Uh…yes, everything is fine now."

Susan desperately wanted to be with her lover once again, so she came back to be able to see him once more.

"Well, that's good," said Mrs. Bryant with a smile. Just then, Jennifer came back to the room, seeing Dr. Bob storm out of the room in tears and sniffing. She wanted to make sure everything was alright.
"Oh!" she said with a startle. "Your back!"

"Yes, Jen. I can take over now," said Susan.

"But…I thought…" said Jennifer with confusion.

"Dear," said Mrs. Bryant to Jennifer, "can you excuse us for just a moment?"

"Oh…um…sure," said Jennifer, who walked out with total confusion on her face.

"Susan," asked Mrs. Bryant, whose smile suddenly disappeared, "why did you come back?"

Trying to act like nothing happened, Susan said, "To finish my shift with Dr. Bryant. I want to take care of him. He has been very good to me, and I want to return the favor as best I can."

Mrs. Bryant walked up to Susan and said, "Really? That's very dedicated, my dear."

Susan smiled and turned away from her in feigned embarrassment, "Thanks."

"Tell me, Susan. Was he good?" Sarah looked at her mother with a look of total confusion at the question. Susan, for her part, froze in fear.

"Excuse me, Mrs. Bryant?" asked Susan, again feigning confusion at her question.

"Was he good?"

Susan didn't answer, but could not look at her face.

"Did he...make you feel good?"

No answer.

"Did he...make you feel *special*? Like you were the only one in the world he cared about?" Mrs. Bryant's eyes narrowed, almost sinisterly, as she spoke these words. Sarah became frozen in shock.

Starting to panic, Susan said, "I...I don't know what you're talking about."

"You know *exactly* what I'm talking about...you unbelievable bitch." Sarah's eyes widened as she looked at her mother after she said this.

"You think you're the only one?" said Mrs. Bryant scoffing. "You think you are the only woman my husband has slept with? You think you are the love of his life?"

Mrs. Bryant walks right up to Susan's face, and Susan backs up a bit, feeling tremendously uncomfortable.

"You are just the latest of his...what did he call them?...Oh, yes, 'interns.'"

Susan was shocked that Mrs. Bryant knew that he called his mistresses his "interns." She thought that was their little secret. She looked at Mrs. Bryant with wide eyes.

"You meant nothing to him...just like all the others. Soon, after he was tired of you, he was planning to throw you away like the rest of his whores."

Her words were like knives cutting her heart in pieces.

"Did you guys fuck on our anniversary?"

Sarah was beside herself in total shock. Susan started to cry and could not look at either of them.

"I heard you on the phone."

"Did you think you were *smart?*" she said sarcastically. "That you could pull one off on the old lady?"

Susan didn't answer.

"Answer me!"

Susan didn't answer.

"You meant nothing to him. At the end of the day, he always came home to *me*. He will always be *mine*. You hear that, bitch? Mine!"

"He loved me!" Susan blurted out in the midst of her grief at Mrs. Bryant's words.

"He loved you as much as he loved his shoes! You were nothing to him, bitch! You hear me? Nothing."

Susan started to sob, holding her head in her hands.

"Get out, you fucking whore! Get out of my husband's room, and don't ever come near my family again!"

Susan stood there frozen and sobbing.

"Get…out!!!"

The force of her voice startled several people in the ICU, including Dr. Sanders, who came into the room when he heard the commotion. He was shocked to see Susan sobbing.

"Is everything OK?" he asked confusedly. "Susan? What's wrong?"

Susan turned away from Dr. Sanders and continued to cry.

"I was asking Ms. Montgomery to leave. I do not want her coming near my husband."

"Is something wrong, ma'am?"

Mrs. Bryant chuckled in angry shock. "Yes, Doctor, something is very wrong, here. I do not want that woman, who has been sleeping with my husband, to come near him."

Dr. Sander's eyes widened in complete shock as he heard those words and looked at Susan intently.

"What?"

"Yes, Doctor. I think it is highly inappropriate for *that woman* to even be in the same vicinity as my husband. Please see to it that she never sees him again."

Dr. Sanders doesn't know what to say, as feelings of deep hurt and deep anger compete for dominance.

"Have I made myself clear, sir?" said Mrs. Bryant more forcefully.

Shaken out of his trance, Dr. Sanders says, "Uh...yes...ma'am. You are abundantly clear." Turning to Susan, he said, "Uh...Susan, I think it is best you leave."

Susan, still sobbing, leaves quietly. Dr. Sanders follows her out of the room.

"Hey!" says Dr. Sanders, grabbing hold of Susan's arm as she is trying to run out of the ICU. He turns her towards him, a little forcefully. His eyes were, again, full of anger and hurt simultaneously.

"Is this true?"

Susan couldn't look her former fiancé in the eyes.

"Is this true?" he asked matter-of-factly.

Susan didn't answer.

"Susie, answer me!"

She didn't answer, although a deep twinge of pain and

guilt flowed through her body when he called her "Susie."

"Is this why you left?...For *him*?"

Susan remained silent, looking at the ground and crying.

"Do you love him?" The question startled Susan a little, and she looked up at Dr. Sanders. She still didn't answer.

"Do you love him?" he repeated, this time more forcefully. She still couldn't answer.

His rage and hurt only increased with her silence, and he turned and walked away, leaving her standing alone. Her crying only increased, and she turned and ran out of the ICU.

Dr. Sanders went back into Dr. Bryant's ICU room with a look of immense anger on his face. He kept looking at Dr. Bryant with anger, ruminating over how this man in the ICU bed, who he is supposed to try to keep alive, seduced his fiancé and took her away from him.

"Dr. Sanders," said Mrs. Bryant with a startled look on her face. "What ever is the matter?" Her words startled him out of his trance of rage.

"Uh...it's been a rough day in the ICU," lied Dr. Sanders.

"Wow," said Mrs. Bryant consolingly.

"How are you, ma'am?" he said, trying to make some small talk.

"I'm ok, doctor. Just in shock by what has all happened."

"Yes, I understand," said Dr. Sanders curtly. "And you, Sarah, is everything OK?"

Sarah nodded silently.

"Mrs. Bryant," said Dr. Sanders, trying to forget about his anger and hurt.

"Have you had any more thoughts about Dr. Bryant's condition? About what he would have wanted in this situation?"

Mrs. Bryant was taken aback and then quickly angered at his question.

"I thought we already had this discussion, doctor. I want everything done for him! Everything!" said Mrs. Bryant.

"Mrs. Bryant..."

"Are you trying to kill my husband? Do you not want to save his life? Isn't that your mission? To save lives, doctor?"

"Yes, of course it is, Mrs. Bryant," said Dr. Sanders.

He was a bit annoyed at that question. He dedicated his whole life, his whole being, to helping alleviate suffering and pain. It is part of this desire that makes him hate to see patients' suffering be prolonged by invasive medical care that he knows to be ultimately futile; patients like Dr. Bryant. He was trying extremely hard to bury his feelings of intense rage and anger at what he did with his former fiancé.

"Then, save my husband's life, Goddamit!" screamed Mrs. Bryant. Sarah was taken aback, but didn't say anything.

"Your husband is dying, Mrs. Bryant. Anything I do is ultimately futile. All it will accomplish is to prolong his pain and suffering," said Dr. Sanders.

"How dare you?! How dare you say that taking care of my husband is futile?" yelled Mrs. Bryant.

"Mrs. Bryant," said Dr. Sanders looking right into her eyes, "nothing is going to help your husband cure his cancer. His brain is probably damaged beyond repair. He will likely not come off the ventilator. He will likely not walk out of this hospital. All we are doing is futile."

Mrs. Bryant could not continue to look back at him, and she turned away, "I don't care. I want everything done," she said, looking out the window into the city. The sun was gleaming brightly against the shiny, steel buildings.

"Mrs. Bryant, are you keeping him alive in revenge?"

"What did you say?" said Sarah, who was heretofore silent. Mrs. Bryant looked at Dr. Sanders in sheer horror.

"Are you keeping him alive so that he will suffer? So that he can feel some of the pain you feel at his betrayal? His repeated betrayals?"

Dr. Sanders deeply regretted uttering that sentence, but it came out in anger. Mrs. Bryant was surprised that he also knew about her husband's multiple affairs.

"How dare you?!" screamed Mrs. Bryant.

With that, Dr. Sanders turned around and walked out of the room, in shock that he actually said what he just said.

Mrs. Bryant was breathing heavily at what Dr. Sanders just said. Dr. Sanders' last statement, though, did make her look at her husband with a bit more disdain, and the desire to make him suffer for what he did to her (and to Sarah) did cross her mind, which frightened her deeply.

"Mom," said Sarah, startling Mrs. Bryant out of her thoughts.

"Did you hear what Dr. Sanders was saying?"

"What?" asked Mrs. Bryant in shock.

"Did you hear what he was saying?"

"Yes, that I am somehow keeping your father alive in revenge for what he has done," said Mrs. Bryant indignantly.

"No, no, no," said Sarah. "That what is being done to Dad is futile; that maybe, we are doing the wrong thing by keeping him alive on all these machines." She said that while pointing her finger at her father, hooked up to all the machines and IV pumps. He was barely recognizable. Mrs. Bryant looked at her husband too, and at that moment, she realized that the man in that bed looked so differently from the man she was with at the dinner just last night.

"Mom, maybe Dad did not want this to be done to him. Maybe, Dad would have wanted us to just make him comfortable if this situation ever came up. I mean, what is better? Simply living, even if it means on a breathing machine, hooked up to all those tubes? Or, does quality of life matter at all?"

Mrs. Bryant sat motionless as Sarah talked.

"I mean, can Dad talk to us? Take a walk with us? Take us out to dinner? Watch the Superbowl with us? Can he do anything fatherly or husbandly like this?"

As she said those words, she thought to herself: *Not that Dad would ever do any of those things with us...*

Mrs. Bryant looked at her husband once again but did not speak.

"True, Dad can't hurt us anymore..."

Mrs. Bryant's almost snapped as she looked at Sarah in disbelief.

"Mom," said Sarah looking straight into her eyes, "Dad hurt the both of us...all of us, including Bobby. We all have to come to terms with that."

Mrs. Bryant looked away and started to cry.

"But, your father loved *me*," said Mrs. Bryant crying, "he would always come back home to *me*. How can I give up on him now? How can Dr. Sanders give up on him, the VIP of this hospital?"

"Mom, I don't think Dr. Sanders is trying to give up on Dad. But, he clearly sees that Dad has come to the end of the road, and he wants him to be made comfortable, without any undue suffering."

Mrs. Bryant then looked at Sarah with disbelief and anger.

"You want your father to die, don't you?" she said.

"No, Mom, no," she said, starting to cry. "I just don't want Dad to suffer." She was really hurt by what her mother had just said.

"How could you say that, Mom? Yes, Dad did terrible things to me...," and with those words she paused a bit looking out into space.

"But, seeing him like this," she said looking again at her father in the ICU bed, "makes me take what Dr. Sanders just said to heart a little."

Mrs. Bryant looked at her daughter with shock.

"How can you agree with that...that...doctor of death Sanders? I want everything done!"

"OK, Mom, OK," said Sarah sniffing and wiping her tears. They proceeded to spend the next hour or so looking in opposite directions, not speaking to one another.

18

"Thanks," said Sarah, another ICU nurse, as she walked out of the ICU to go to the bathroom. As soon she opened the door, she became instantly pale...and no longer needed to go to the bathroom. She gasped and put her hands over her mouth, barely able to breathe at what she was seeing. With each gasp came a sob as well, and she stumbled back outside the bathroom to try to get help. She missed the push plate to her left several times before finally connecting with it to open the doors. As the doors opened, she was able to muster enough strength to scream, "Help! Call a Code Blue!"

Denise was standing close enough to the doors to hear Sarah's panicked screams for help.

"What's wrong?" asked Denise.

"Call a code blue!" screamed Sarah.

"What happened?" asked Denise, again, this time a bit more alarmed.

"Someone's dying in the bathroom! Get Dr. Sanders!" screamed Sarah, again.

"Oh my God!" gasped Denise, and she quickly picked up the phone and dialed the extension to which all "code blues" are called.

"We have a code blue outside of the ICU. Yes, outside of the ICU. Thanks."

A few moments later, a loud voice blared over the hospital PA system, "Code blue...ICU. Code Blue...ICU. Code blue...ICU."

Dr. Sanders heard the announcement and came running to the nurses station with the fellow and senior resident.

"What's going on?" he asked in alarm. "Who's coding?"

"Someone is dying in the women's bathroom," said Denise. She was much more calm and collected than Sarah, who was bent over crying and hyperventilating outside of the women's bathroom outside of the ICU. Yet, Denise did not behold the grisly scene inside the bathroom...yet.

Dr. Sanders, along with the fellow and senior resident, walked quickly to the large doors and pushed the plate to open them. When they opened, he saw Sarah nearly collapsed on the floor, crying.

"What's wrong, Sarah?" Dr. Sander's asked.

All Sarah could do was point to the bathroom. Dr. Sanders then burst into the bathroom, and he had to step back at what he saw, gasping in sheer horror.

Susan was unconscious on the floor in a large pool of blood; it was most of her blood volume, in fact. Dr. Sanders immediately reached down and felt for her pulse on her neck. There was none. He then kneeled down in the pool of blood to her right side in order to do CPR. He yelled out, "Get the intubation kit!" The senior resident ran back inside the ICU to get a gray tackle box filled with supplies to place an artificial breathing tube in her throat. Susan was clearly not breathing.

By this time, a whole cadre of people had arrived from all parts of the hospital to help out in the code. They were quite relaxed, because most of them figured that some old lady fainted, and this whole thing will be much ado about nothing. How wrong they all were, and when they each beheld the ghastly scene of Dr. Sanders administering CPR in a pool of blood, they were shocked to the very core.

"Do you have an Ambu bag?" yelled Dr. Sanders frantically. An "Ambu bag" is a device that helps artificially breathe for a patient who has stopped breathing on their own. The respiratory therapist, John, walked up to the opposite side of Dr. Sanders, a little hesitantly because of the sheer volume of her blood on the floor. Dr. Sanders also hated being in her blood, but he swallowed his anxiety to help Susan. As he was doing CPR, he was devastated and had no small amount of guilt.

"Bag her!" yelled Dr. Sanders frantically. Sweat was beginning to pour down his face as he continued to do CPR. John placed a clear plastic mask attached to a big plastic balloon filled with air on her mouth and nose. He then held the mask tightly to her face with one hand while squeezing the balloon with the other hand, forcing much needed air into Susan's lungs. A large crowd was now gathered outside the bathroom. More would have been inside, but everyone was afraid of the blood.

"Do you want me to take over, Dr. Sanders?" asked Dr. Ahmed.

"No, just tube her," said Dr. Sanders, sweating and breathing quickly. CPR was an excellent workout, one that few like to do.

Just then the senior resident came back with the intubation box. Dr. Ahmed took it from him and opened it up. Inside were a number of supplies: plastic breathing tubes, curved and straight metal objects that looked like swords, with a light on the end, to help keep the airway open. Those blades, as they are called, are attached to a metal cylinder, which is a handle and houses the batteries that supply the light on the end of the blade. There are also spare batters, carbon dioxide detectors, to help tell the doctor that the tube is actually in the lung, rather than the stomach. Placing the breathing tube in the stomach is very easy to do...and can be devastating to the patient if not detected immediately. There were also long, thin plastic tubes, almost like pipe cleaners, that go into the breathing tubes to help stiffen them. This helps the person placing the tube, called "intubating," insert it into the windpipe much more easily.

Dr. Ahmed took what he needed from the box and set everything up quickly. He then stepped over Dr. Sanders to get to her head, and he connected the curved blade to the metal handle. Placing the curved blade into her mouth, he lifted the handle up to get a clear view of her vocal cords. He then picked up the breathing tube and placed it into her lungs. He knew he was in, because he saw the tube going through the vocal cords. Dr. Ahmed then connected the tube to the Ambu bag and began breathing for her. There was a small device attached to a side port of the Ambu bag. It contained a purple paper inside which turned yellow every time she exhaled. It is the carbon dioxide detector, and that color change confirmed for Dr. Ahmed and Dr. Sanders that the tube was in the right organ.

"Nice job, dude," said Dr. Sanders.

"Thanks, Dr. Sanders," said Dr. Ahmed. Inside, he was beaming with satisfaction. It is always nice to do a good job in front of your boss, especially when it comes to intubation. Intubation can be very tricky, even for the most experienced of physicians.

"Dr. Sanders," said Dr. Ahmed. "Please, let me take over doing compressions."

Dr. Sanders stopped and felt for Susan's pulse. Nothing. He wanted to continue to be the "big boss" and do CPR. But, acquiesced to his fellow, because, he was exhausted. John, the respiratory therapist, took over breathing for Susan.

"Sure," he said, secretly relieved at his fellow making the suggestion.

Now that he was free of the arduous task of CPR, Dr. Sanders was able to get up off the floor, his scrubs soaked in blood, and assess the situation. Immediately, he realized the cause of her likely death.

"She slit her wrists," said Dr. Sanders, and his eyes began to well up with tears. Everyone around them let out a quite gasp.

"My God," said Dr. Sanders, barely able to speak through his tears and guilt. Some of the large crowd now gathered could be heard crying.

"Get a cart, we need to take her into the ICU right away," said Dr. Sanders. With that, one of the observers dashed into the ICU and quickly came back with a cart. The ICU doors have been propped open by the security guards who responded to the code, trying to keep order outside, but desperately trying to see what's going on inside. People made way for the cart, and both Dr. Sanders and Dr. Ahmed lifted

Susan onto the cart and rushed her into an empty ICU room. Dr. Ahmed was on the cart giving CPR as they carefully wheeled her into the room.

At that moment, Sarah and Mrs. Bryant peaked out of ICU Room 7. They were taken aback at what they saw: the cart being wheeled, with Dr. Ahmed administering CPR, into an ICU room.

"What happened?" asked Mrs. Bryant to Denise, who was standing at the nurses station motionless and crying.

"One of the nurses was found in the bathroom unconscious. It seems she tried to kill herself by slitting her wrists," said Denise, sniffing, crying, and wiping her tears.

"Oh my dear, precious Lord!" exclaimed Mrs. Bryant.

As Sarah and her mother stood in shock, other nurses were quickly placing monitors on Susan's arms and chest. The monitor read a flat line: no heart activity. Dr. Sanders quickly placed a special IV in the main vein of Susan's groin, in order to administer powerful drugs to help jumpstart her heart. They gave her shocks, and CPR, and drugs. They pushed in a massive amount of blood into her body. They bandaged her wrists very tightly. They worked on her for more than an hour. But, there was nothing. It was too late. Susan had bled too much, too quickly. It was over.

"OK, everybody," said Dr. Sanders, barely able to

speak, "there's...there's nothing more we can do. Time...," he couldn't stop the tears, "time...of...death...is 12:25."

The nurses all stood in their places, frozen with intense grief, each of them crying. In fact, the entire ICU stood frozen, unable to believe that Susan, one of their own, had just committed suicide underneath all of their noses.

"What is going on?" asked Mrs. Bryant to Denise again.

"Susan Montgomery, one of the ICU nurses," said Denise crying, "just died."

Sarah and Mrs. Bryant both gasped simultaneously. Mrs. Bryant didn't know what to feel: indeed, she was sad that she died – she had no intention of making her feel so bad as to kill herself – but she was also extremely angry at her brazenness, her gall at trying to be with her lover in front of his wife. Yet, soon, these mixed feelings changed into anger, and she walked back into her husband's room.

As soon as she walked into the room, Mrs. Bryant walked up slowly to her husband's head and whispered softly into his ear.

"Your fucking whore is dead," said Mrs. Bryant softly, and after a pause she added: "you unbelievable fucking bastard."

Mrs. Bryant lifted up her head, but then paused and

went back down to say one more thing to her husband.

"But, I am still here, because I love you, and I want to be here at your side in your darkest hour. I knew about all of your other…'interns,' Billy. But, I knew that you still loved me. That's why I remained silent all these years."

After another pause, she added: "But, I will never forgive both you…and…myself for what you did to Bobby and Sarah."

"How…," said Mrs. Bryant, starting to cry, "how could you…"

19

Dr. Sanders sat at the desk at the nurses' station in total shock, not able to say anything while sniffing and wiping back endless tears. Most of the other staff members were doing the same thing. No one could believe what just happened.

"Joe?" asked a voice that startled him, causing him to look up suddenly. His alarm went away when he saw his old friend, Dr. Bob. Yet, it came right back when he saw his appearance. His eyes widened when he saw his friend.

He looked absolutely terrible: large, dark circles under his eyes; his hair was completely disheveled, and his scrubs looked old and equally disheveled. Anyone looking at him could not help but feel enormous pity.

"Bob! Dude...what the hell happened to you?" asked Dr. Sanders in shock.

"I've...I've had a bad couple of days."

"Susan just killed herself."

"What?!" asked Dr. Bob in feeble shock that looked more like disinterested surprise. "How? What happened?"

"Apparently, she slit her wrists in the bathroom right outside. Underneath all of our noses. She...she exsanguinated before we could..."

Dr. Sanders' voice trailed off in a stream of tears. Dr. Bob tried to show some emotion, but he simply could not. He stood there as stoic as ever and said:

"Can I see my Dad?"

Dr. Sanders was a little put off by his lack of emotion, but he didn't want to get into a confrontation at this point.

"Sure. Your mother and sister are in there with him."

"Thanks," he said, and he walked into the ICU room. Dr. Sanders' looked at his friend in astonishment at his reaction.

He walked into the room silently, and both Sarah and Mrs. Bryant didn't notice that he came in. His hands were shaking, and he was sniffing almost constantly, and this sniff made them turn around. Once again, their eyes widened at the sight of their family member.

"Bobby!" exclaimed Sarah.

"Oh my God! Son? Are you alright?" asked his mother, who was clearly taken aback by his appearance. He did not answer her question, but looked at his mother.

"Please, son, please, sit down here," said Mrs. Bryant, moving away from her chair to let him sit in it. In her heart, she wanted him to sit down in the chair, and then she would rub his hair, like she used to do when he was much younger. She wanted desperately to comfort him, which is something she had not done for many, many years.

"No, mother. I'm fine right here," he said stoically.

"Bobby, honey, please," she said walking up to her son, "come and sit down with us. Come be with your sister...who has come back to us...from the dead," she said pleadingly.

"It's good to see you again, Bobby," said Sarah, a little hesitantly. Dr. Bob glanced at his sister with a brief, but powerful look of sheer pain and sadness. She immediately understood the pain and agony he was having, and it overwhelmed his sister. She ran to him, sobbing, and embraced her brother tightly. The tears were streaming down her face and wetting his scrubs. He didn't reach out at first, but then he embraced his sister equally as tightly. He wanted to sob out loud; he wanted to scream out loud; he wanted to tell his sister how happy he was to see her, even though he said she was "dead" to him.

He didn't. He just embraced her tightly, with tears streaming down his face as well. Their mother was so touched by this spectacle, and she stood crying silently. The embrace was quite long, and Sarah did not want it to end. Although they said no words, they had the most profound conversation a brother and sister who have been abused by their father could ever have. But, suddenly, Dr. Bob pushed his sister away from him, to her shock and sadness.

"NO!" said Dr. Bob loudly, and he stepped back and pulled out a 9mm handgun from his back.

Both Mrs. Bryant and Sarah screamed loudly, and this alerted Dr. Sanders, who came into the room running. He froze in terror when he saw Dr. Bob standing with a gun pointed at his mother.

"Don't move another inch, Mother! And…and," he said with growing rage and clenched teeth, "don't call me Bobby!"

"Bob…calm down, OK?" said Dr. Sanders, still frozen in place.

"No, you calm down!" said Dr. Bob, now pointing the gun at his friend. Dr. Sanders shuddered in total fear.

"Please, Bob. Please…don't do this, man."

"Son? Why are you doing this?"

Dr. Bob kept moving the gun between his mother and Dr. Sanders.

They all became startled by the overhead page that suddenly appeared: "CODE SILVER, ICU. CODE SILVER, ICU. CODE SILVER, ICU." A "Code Silver" indicates someone with a weapon.

"Why don't I just end it now, huh? It's all *his* fault! It's…it's all…," he begins to cry with rage, "it's all HIS FAULT." With that, he points the gun at his father.

"NO!" screams Sarah, who has been heretofore frozen in terror and shock. She almost leaps and places herself over her father's body, shocking everyone in the room, including Dr. Bob.

"Bobby! No! This is our father…" she said, crying and sobbing out loud. "No matter what…he is still…he is still our fath…" She couldn't complete her sentence.

"After what he did to you?" he asked in total rage and shock. "After what he did to me? To Mom? To…to all of us?" His rage made him point his gun even more at his father.

"He is still our father, Bobby. Don't destroy your life. We need you…I…I need you…" said Sarah, crying.

When she said that, his eyes widened and welled up further with tears. No one has ever told him that they needed him. When Sarah said that, it made him hesitate ever slightly, and his grip on the gun began to weaken a little.

Suddenly, three frantic and armed security guards burst into the room, all guns pointed at Dr. Bob:

"DROP YOUR WEAPON!"
"DROP YOUR WEAPON NOW, DOCTOR!"
"DOCTOR, DROP YOUR WEAPON!"

The security guards were all extremely nervous, although it did not seem that way to an outside observer. Dr. Bob, still with his gun pointed at his father and sister, looked completely confused. His hands were shaking, and blood began to seep through his bandaged hand.

Looking at his mother, then his sister – who stood up from covering her father – Dr. Bob pointed the gun at his own head, to the frantic shrieks of his mother.

"Bobby! Don't do it! Don't do it!"

"DROP YOUR WEAPON!" continued to be blurted out by the security guards, guns still pointed at him.

Sarah was sobbing, and she said to him, pleading: "Bobby…don't do this…don't leave…"

"Doctor, please, calm down. Please, doctor, drop your gun and relax," said one security guard, realizing that a tough tone may actually be worse, putting out his hand to the other guards, motioning them to be silent.

Dr. Bob took in what was happening, and he pointed the gun more forcefully at his own head, to the screams of his frantic family.

"Please, doctor, please. Don't do this. Put down your gun, and let's talk about this," said the guard in a calming voice.

He looked at his mother and sister one more time and then pulled the trigger.

20

The bang startled everyone in the room, and they all ducked for cover in sheer terror. Dr. Bob was on the ground convulsing, with blood all over his face and the floor.

"Oh my God! Oh my God!" Mrs. Bryant kept screaming as she was crouched on the ground holding Sarah as tightly as she could. Dr. Sanders was also on the ground in sheer terror and panic, but he was able to see that Dr. Bob was seizing violently on the ground.

At the exact same time, the monitor that was keeping track of Dr. Bryant's vital signs began to alarm as the oxygen level began to go down, with the blood pressure going up.

Dr. Sanders got up, realizing that the danger has passed, and assessed the situation: both father and son are critically ill. So, he ran to the phone in the room and dialed the switchboard:

"Yes, this is Dr. Sanders. Please call the Code Silver all clear and call a Code Blue....I know the Police are supposed to do it, but this is an emergency!"

"Call a Code Blue!!!" he screamed and slams down the phone.

The security guard has now gotten up and secured Dr. Bob's weapon so it does not go off again accidentally.

When no overhead page came, Dr. Sanders reached for the switch on the wall at the head of the bed labeled "CODE" and pulled it. The alarms blared, and soon afterwards an overhead page was heard: "CODE BLUE, ICU. CODE BLUE, ICU. CODE BLUE, ICU."

As soon as that page came, the SWAT team, fully dressed in combat gear, burst into the ICU and secured the entire area. The security guards went out of the ICU room to meet them, and they filled them in on the details.

Meanwhile, Dr. Sanders screamed out of the room: "I NEED HELP!!! PLEASE HELP!!!"

A number of residents and staff, as well as Dr. Ahmed, were hiding all over the ICU. When they heard Dr. Sanders' frantic cries for help, they got up and looked around. Seeing the SWAT team there, they felt safe enough to come out. They heard the

CODE BLUE, but they were too scared to come and help.

"HELP!!!" came another scream from Dr. Sanders. Sarah and Mrs. Bryant were in the corner of the room, horrified and sobbing.

Dr. Ahmed and a bunch of other residents and staff came into the room and were shocked by what they saw.

"Dr. Sanders, what happened?" screamed Dr. Ahmed.

"Dr. Bob shot himself. Mohamed, take care of Dr. Bob!"

Dr. Ahmed sprung into action, yelling out, "I need an intubation tray now! He then went to Dr. Bob and laid him on his side.

"Give some 10mg of Ativan now!" screamed Dr. Ahmed.

By now, more staff had entered into the ICU room, and one of them dashed outside to get him the medication he requested. Someone else came to the room with the red ICU "crash cart," where all the life-saving drugs are kept to be used during a cardiac arrest.

Suddenly, Dr. Bryant also started seizing violently.

Dr. Sanders yelled out, "Ah, God dammit!"

Meanwhile, Dr. Ahmed was holding on to the still seizing younger Bryant.

"Where's my Ativan?!" he screamed again. Ativan is a tranquilizer that works to stop seizures when they happen. In a few moments, a nurse came running in with a syringe of clear fluid.

"Ativan, Dr. Ahmed," she said. He grabbed it from her hand and quickly injected it into his arm. A few minutes later, his seizure began to subside, but he was clearly not breathing.

"Get me an Ambu bag! Get a 7.5 ET tube ready! Can someone come and put in a line?" yelled Dr. Ahmed. Another nurse came along with an IV kit to try and start an IV. When she pulled back the long sleeve undershirt off his arm, she was taken aback.

"Oh my God!" said the nurse. "He has track marks everywhere! I think he's been abusing IV drugs."

"Oh, man. Try to get anything. I have to intubate him. We need to get him to an ICU room. My God!" gasped Dr. Ahmed.

Dr. Ahmed then proceeded to place a breathing tube in Dr. Bob's windpipe.

"Ativan for me, also!" screamed Dr. Sanders, tending to Dr. Bryant the father. The nurse who gave Dr. Ahmed his Ativan left and quickly came back with another syringe of clear fluid.

"Ativan, Dr. Sanders," she said.

Dr. Sanders injected it quickly into Dr. Bryant's IV line, and as he looked up at the monitor, he exclaimed in exasperation: "Oh shit!"

The monitor showed that Dr. Bryant's heart had stopped and his oxygen and blood pressure have gone to zero.

"CPR! Start CPR!" screamed Dr. Sanders. Another resident quickly jumped on the bed and started giving CPR to the father.

"What the hell is going on here?" yelled Dr. Frank, who burst into the room to see what had happened in the ICU. Once the Code Silver was cleared, someone from the ICU called him to let him know of the situation. When he saw the younger Bryant, in a pool of blood, seizing and the older Bryant on the bed seizing, he stepped back in shock and terror.

"My God!"

"Bobby shot himself, and he is now seizing. Now, Dr. Bryant is seizing."

"What can I do?" asked Dr. Frank, leaping into action.

"Try to get Bobby into a cart and a room, so we can hook him up."

"We need a cart in here STAT!" he screamed to

anyone outside.

Almost immediately, someone came in with a bed, and Drs. Ahmed and Frank along with the nurse who came in lifted the limp son onto the bed and wheeled him to the ICU room next door, which happened to be empty. They hooked him up to the monitor and started IVs.

At the same time, Dr. Sanders was yelling out orders to give various medicines to the ailing father, who was still seizing.

All the while stood Sarah and her mother, too in shock to say anything, horrified by what they have just witnessed. Just then, Mrs. Bryant let out a scream, and Sarah immediately grabbed her mother and hugged her tightly, muffling the repeated screams she made into her shirt. As she stood there consoling her mother, the tears and sobs flowed continuously down Sarah's face.

21

"God damn it, stop seizing!" screamed Dr. Frank.

"Get the pentothal and propofol! Snow him until he doesn't move!" screamed Dr. Frank again. After a few moments, a nurse came into the room with two vials of medication, one was clear, and one looked like milk.

"How much, doctor?" asked the nurse. As he was about to give her the dose, a frantic voice screamed from outside the room.

"Just give it all!" he screamed again, with a scowl that could kill to the nurse. She shuddered a bit, and started to draw up the medicines in a syringe. She was so nervous, her hands were shaking violently.

Meanwhile, next door, Dr. Bryant the father had stopped seizing, but that was because his heart had stopped pumping.

"Stop CPR," said Dr. Sanders, completely exhausted, scrubs covered in dried blood. The sweaty resident doing CPR stopped, grateful for the break. Someone else then tapped him on the shoulder to take his place.

"What's the underlying rhythm?" asked Dr. Sanders.

"Asystole," someone blurted out.

"Continue CPR," said Dr. Sanders, now with a little angry annoyance at this hopeless situation. He took a look at the corner of the room to behold Sarah and Mrs. Bryant. His initial look was of angry disdain, but when he saw Mrs. Bryant sobbing in Sarah's arms, his demeanor softened a little.

Suddenly, however, his face took a look of indignant anger, and he clenched his fists tightly.

"Stop."

Everyone looked at Dr. Sanders with a look of complete and utter terror. After a few seconds, the resident continued CPR, thinking that he had misheard Dr. Sanders for sure.

"I said stop!" yelled Dr. Sanders more loudly.

The resident was completely confused, saying: "Dr. Sanders, he is a full code. What do you mean stop?"

"This is completely futile. He is not going to survive.

He is NOT going to walk out of this hospital alive. I am putting an end to this madness. Stop CPR! No epi! No atropine!" said Dr. Sanders, putting out his arm to the equally shocked nurses in the room.

The alarms on the monitor were screaming, and Sarah and her mother were sobbing and watching the situation with eyes wide in utter shock. One of the staff quickly went next door and told Dr. Frank what was happening. He came running into the room in a made rage.

"WHAT ARE YOU DOING?" screamed Dr. Frank.

"Dr. Frank, I said stop CPR. This is futile care. He is not going to survive this."

Dr. Frank looked at Dr. Sanders dumbfounded, and after a few seconds he blurted out: "You're crazy!"

Dr. Frank motioned to the resident to continue CPR: "Continue CPR. Give another dose of Epi."

"NO!" screamed Dr. Sanders. "STOP CPR!"

"Just keep going," said Dr. Frank, moving to ignore a clearly insane (in his mind) Dr. Sanders.

After a few moments, Dr. Sanders then moved and pushed the resident off Dr. Bryant's chest, who fell to the floor and let out a yell of pain.

"What are you doing?"!" screamed Dr. Frank. He moved to get Dr. Sanders out of the room, but Dr.

Sanders then punched him hard in the abdomen. Dr. Frank bent over, not being able to breathe. Sarah screamed, and another staff member went to get security to help the situation.

As Dr. Frank was bent over, trying to recover from the blow to his abdomen, Dr. Sanders then turned to the monitor and watched as it continued to be a flat line. No rhythm ever returned. Dr. Bryant made no motion; he made no independent respiratory effort.

"Time of death, 4:35 PM," said Dr. Sanders coldly. He then proceeded to take off his gloves as everyone in the room looked at him completely dumbfounded.

"What have you done?" screamed an incredulous Mrs. Bryant.

"Your husband is dead, Mrs. Bryant. We did everything we could," said Dr. Sanders.

"You gave up on him!" screamed Sarah, tears streaming down her face. "Who gave you the right to determine who lives and who dies? We wanted everything done! How dare you?"

"You killed my husband!" screamed Mrs. Bryant and she lunged for Dr. Sanders, but because of what has all happened, she was extremely weak, and she fell straight to the ground. Sarah let out a scream and bent down to prevent her mother from falling on the floor and hurting herself. Dr. Sanders stood motionless as he watched Mrs. Bryant almost fall to the ground in front of him.

At this time, two security guards and a police officer came into the room, and Dr. Frank was able to let out a command, still gasping from the blow to his abdomen:

"Arrest Dr. Sanders at once! He has assaulted me, and I want to press full charges."

The police officer moved to restrain Dr. Sanders, and he resisted, but this made the officer very angry.

"Sir, stop resisting arrest," he said very annoyed.

"I did nothing wrong, Dr. Frank. This was futile care, and you know it."

"Take this man to my office, please. I need to talk to him first, and then you can take him away."

"Let go of me!" yelled Dr. Sanders, still fighting.

"Sir, stop resisting, or I will have to pull out the Taser." At that, Dr. Sanders stopped fighting the officer, and let the officer restrain him.

As Sarah was holding her mother, she could not stand up, so she let her mother sit gently on the floor for a few moments before she could gather her strength to get her back up. Mrs. Bryant was sobbing uncontrollably, and Sarah looked straight into the eyes of Dr. Sanders as she was holding her mother.

Then, Sarah said in a slow and methodical manner:

"What sort of monster are you?"

Dr. Sanders looked at her and, as they were taking him away, said, "I am very sorry for your loss." He had no emotion on his face.

Amid a totally silent ICU, except for the "whoosh" of air from a number of ventilators and the beeps of various monitors, Dr. Sanders was led out of the ICU in handcuffs as everyone watched in total shock. No one could believe what had just transpired here.

The screams of Sarah and Mrs. Bryant brought out the staff in Dr. Bob's room. When his nurse realized that she was supposed to give him medicines to stop his seizures, she rushed back into the room only to be shocked by what she discovered.

Despite having seized for more than half an hour, almost continuously, Dr. Bob stopped seizing on his own. His vital signs, which were completely erratic before, normalized. Even though he was on a ventilator and hooked up to tubes, he looked more at peace at that moment than he had in years.

Taking advantage of the lull in the ICU, an officer came into his room and placed a handcuff on one of his wrists, with the other cuff connected to the bedrail.

22

The post-cry sniffing ceased to stop, and it was the only sound in the ICU room in which Dr. Bob was laying, as peaceful as ever, on the ventilator and connected to tubes. Mrs. Bryant and Sarah were at his bedside, sitting quietly, with Mrs. Bryant holding his hand. The day was getting late, and the bright orange light of a setting May sun was beaming into the room, just hugging Dr. Bryant's body. The chaos that was in the ICU had died down, but both Sarah and Mrs. Bryant were still in shock at what just happened.

The television in the room was on, and the newscast was discussing the "police incident" at Chicago Memorial Hospital. Rumors were flying all around what really happened, but the Hospital's official statement to the press was that it was a false alarm.

Dr. Bryant the father's body has been taken to the morgue, and arrangements were already being prepared for the funeral. There were still police officers in the ICU, and the room that heretofore held Dr. Bryant had yellow police tape across it, as it now became a crime scene.

Just then, as Mrs. Bryant was concentrating on her son, she let out a gasp.

"Bobby? Bobby? Honey, are you ok?" she asked.

Dr. Bob. opened his eyes and looked around. Mrs. Bryant was already standing when his eyes met hers. He looked directly into them and Mrs. Bryant immediately started crying, gripping his hand even more tightly.

"It's OK, honey. It's OK. Mama's here. Mama's here," she said crying.

When she said that, Dr. Bob was immediately comforted, and a small tear streaked down his face. Mrs. Bryant knew what his look meant, what he was trying to say. That he was crying out for his Mama; that he wanted her comfort right now. It was something he had not had in a very, very long time, but something he had longed for a very, very long time. Mrs. Bryant reached down and kissed her son's forehead, and he closed his eyes out of a relief he hadn't felt in decades.

He then looked into his sister's eyes. Sarah began to cry as well, and she and her mother looked at each other.

"It's OK, Bobby. It's OK. I'm here for you, Bobby.

I'm here for you," said Sarah. She knew what the look was: it was one of deep apology: for cursing her out when she first came; for thinking his sister dead after she ran away and not looking for her; for not defending her more against her father's ravages and abuses. Sarah reached down and kissed his forehead as well.

"Get some rest, Bobby. Get some rest, son. We will be back in the morning," said Mrs. Bryant, in that soothing motherly voice.

Dr. Bob closed his eyes and went back to sleep, getting the best rest he has had in perhaps 15 years, even though he was connected to state of the art, yet uncomfortable, medical equipment. Mrs. Bryant looked at her watch, and realized the late hour. She had a lot of work to do, with the funeral and all.

"It's late. I need to get home. I think Bobby will be OK tonight," she said looking over at her son. "I will be back tomorrow."

"Sarah," said Mrs. Bryant. "Why don't you come home with me? It will be much better for you than that hotel by the airport."

"Oh no, Mother. I don't think so," said Sarah, a bit frightened. Yes, she went to the house looking for her mother, but she didn't have the courage to actually sleep there. Not after what had happened to her.

"Sarah, it's alright. I will be there with you. I can't stay alone tonight. I need you, honey. I need you," said

Mrs. Bryant.

"Mother..."

"Sarah," Mrs. Bryant said forcefully, "you are coming home with me tonight and that's that."

"Well," said Sarah, a bit in a daze, "I need to go back to the hotel and get my things."

"That's no problem, dear. It's on the way home."

"Alright, Mom. You win."

They both got up, and Mrs. Bryant gave her son one more kiss. They then walked out of the ICU, and went downstairs to the first floor. George was still downstairs, faithfully waiting as he always does. He opened the door for the both of them, and they both got into the car.

"Mrs. Bryant! I'm so glad you are OK. I saw the SWAT team come through the front door. Is everything alright?" asked a frightened George.

"We'll talk about it on the way home, George," said an exhausted Mrs. Bryant.

"But first, we need to stop at the hotel at the airport and get Sarah's things. She's staying with me, tonight."

"That's wonderful!" exclaimed George. "It will be so nice to have you back home, my precious Sarah."

Sarah looked at George and smiled, but she was very nervous about going back to her home. Mrs. Bryant held her hand after he said that and smiled as well. It did not take long to get to the airport, and on the way, Sarah and her mother just sat quietly, trying to absorb what had just happened. They told George about the death of Dr. Bryant and what transpired with Dr. Bob and he was speechless at the news. He could not believe that his long time employer - and friend had passed away. He seemed at the top of his game, and now this.

"I will be right out, Mom," said Sarah as they pulled to the front of the hotel.

"We will be here, Sarah," said Mrs. Bryant.

"If you don't come out in five minutes, I'm coming in there after you Sarah, " said George.

Sarah smiled.

As she walked into the lobby, she froze, as if she saw her father standing there before her. But, she didn't see her father, but her husband. He had just arrived from Seattle when she walked into the lobby. She immediately ran into his arms and buried her face in his chest, not able to control her sobs.

"Oh my precious Sarah," said Jonathan. "You didn't answer your phone, and I got so scared. I couldn't be away from you. I didn't know what happened, and I just got so scared."

"Oh, baby. I am so happy you are here. My father is dead. He was so sick, but the doctor refused to revive him. He just let him die."

"Oh my God!"

Of course, that was not the whole story, but she did not have the energy to tell him everything, not just yet. They stood there in the lobby embracing for several minutes. She was so very happy to see him, and it was the best gift she could have ever received at that dark moment in her life. As they stood there arm in arm, Mrs. Bryant came into the lobby looking for Sarah. She became worried.

"Sarah!" she exclaimed. "Are you alright, honey?"

Sarah was startled at the sound of her mother's voice. She turned to see her mother standing there.

"Jonathan, I presume?" asked Mrs. Bryant, smiling. Sarah smiled back, holding her husband tight in her arms.

"Yes, Mom, this is my husband, Jonathan Meyers."

"Pleasure to meet you Mrs. Bryant," said Jonathan, extending his hand to Mrs. Bryant.

"Oh my precious Lord!"

She then extended her hand to his and pulled it toward him.

"Come give me a hug, precious," said Mrs. Bryant. "And call me 'Mom'"

"OK...Mom," said Jonathan a little awkwardly as he embraced his mother-in-law. She then let him go, looking straight at him.

"You are even more gorgeous than I imagined," she said. "Sarah, you do know how to pick 'em."

"Yup," said Sarah proudly. "I hit the jackpot with this one." She was rubbing his shoulder as she said that.

"Come on, get your things. You are coming home with me." said Mrs. Bryant.

"No, ma'am..."

"NO IFs, ANDs, or BUTs about it! You are coming home with me, and that's that!"

"I already tried, honey. Don't even start," said Sarah to her husband.

"Alright," said Jonathan chuckling.

They sent a porter to get Sarah's things from the hotel room and then checked out. As they walked out to the car, George was standing at the door, waiting. Jonathan was amazed at the very expensive car they had.

"George," said Sarah. "This is my husband, Jonathan Meyers."

Jonathan extended his hand saying, "Pleasure to meet you, sir."

"Pleasure is all mine. Man," said George looking at Sarah, "Sarah, you really know how to pick 'em."

Jonathan blushed.

"Yes, I do," said Sarah.

They all got into the car and drove home. They got stuck in traffic, and during that time, Sarah told her husband the events of the day, and he simply sat there in sheer disbelief. Mrs. Bryant sat, speechless, looking out the window at the world passing (slowly) by.

23

"Sit down!" he screamed.

Dr. Sanders was startled by his scream, and he turned around to look at a fuming Dr. Frank as he walked into his office. There was an officer standing beside Dr. Sanders, quietly listening.

"Officer, can you excuse us for a few minutes, please?" asked Dr. Frank.

"No problem, sir," said the officer, who turned to leave. "I will be right outside if you need anything."

"Thank you," said Dr. Frank, turning his attention to Dr. Sanders.

"Hey, what is your problem?" said Dr. Sanders, who was clearly annoyed and angered.

"Don't you say a word to me!" said Dr. Frank, barely

able to control his sheer rage at his young junior associate. "What...where...what just happened in the ICU?"

There was silence.

"Speak!" screamed Dr. Frank.

"Oh, now I am allowed to talk?" asked Dr. Sanders sarcastically. Dr. Frank slammed his fist on his desk, taking Dr. Sanders aback.

"Coding Dr. Bryant was an exercise in futility. He was not going to survive. It was over, and continuing on..."

"Did you not know he was a full code?" quipped Dr. Frank.

"I did, but..."

"So, then how could just stop?"

"It...was...FUTILE!"

"And who gave you the authority to determine this?"

"Actually, state law does, Dr. Frank." Dr. Frank was surprised at this answer.

"I don't give a DAMN what state law says. He was a full code, and our hospital policy – and your moral and ethical obligation – states that you continue on until *he* could not be brought back, not until *you* felt it was useless."

"By coding him for the billionth time, I *was doing him harm*. His wife didn't understand that..."

"And so you killed him to make a point?"

"I DID NOT kill Dr. Bryant!" Dr. Sanders stood up in rage, but he gasped a little from the pain of the handcuffs.

"Tell that to the Bryant family. Do you know what kind of lawsuit they are going to bring against you? Against this hospital?"

Silence.

"Huh, do you? Do you know how badly you have damaged the reputation of this hospital? Do you know what kind of press this is going to bring? Already, I am getting calls from the media. What am I supposed to tell them? My doctor 'got tired' of taking care of the *head* of cardiovascular surgery at his very own hospital? Do you understand what how much trouble you have caused this institution?"

"DO YOU?" screamed Dr. Frank.

"It was futile, I tell you! Futile!"

"And on top of that, you push a resident on the floor? He is liable to sue us as well. My stomach still hurts. What were you thinking?"

Silence.

"You have done more damage in ten minutes than all of Dr. Bryant's shenanigans over the past 25 years. You are on your own, pal. We are not going to take the fall for your stupid decisions. You are dismissed, sir."

Dr. Frank then got up and walked to the door of his office. He opened it up and said, "Officer, you may take him now."

The officer then walked up to Dr. Sanders, who was already standing, and took him by his handcuffed arms.

"Let's go, sir."

"You have not heard the last from me. I will see you in court!" said Dr. Sanders.

"Can't wait," said Dr. Frank, mockingly.

He watched the officer take Dr. Sanders out of his office, and he sat at his desk, intermittently letting out curses to vent his still fuming rage.

24

We regret to inform you of the passing of Dr. L. William Bryant Jr., Chief of Cardiovascular Surgery of Chicago Memorial Hospital. Funeral arrangements are pending and will be announced at the Memorial Service that is to be held today, in the Johnson Conference Center at 5 P.M. Please join us to commemorate the life and achievements of one of our dearest staff members.

This was the nondescript announcement that was posted in the Doctors' Lounge and in the ICU and CCU. They also announced the memorial service in the morning and later on in the afternoon. The announcement only came because one of the hospital chaplains felt compassion for his family. At around 4 P.M., Mrs. Bryant, Sarah, and her husband stopped by Dr. Bob's ICU room to check and see how he was doing. They did not come sooner because they were all simply exhausted from the happenings of the previous day.

It was quite amazing that a memorial service was set up the next day after his death, and it is unclear if this was a sign of great love for the late Chief of Cardiovascular Surgery or a desire to go through the motions and get it over with.

Sarah, Mrs. Bryant, and Jonathan walked into the ICU and everyone simply looked at them with blank stares. Everyone was still in shock at the events of the previous day. Both Sarah and her mother walked quickly, and Jonathan had trouble keeping up.

They were all pleasantly surprised to see Dr. Bob off the machine and breathing on his own. He was resting comfortably with two prongs in his nostrils giving him oxygen. Mrs. Bryant's heart melted when she saw her son resting so comfortably, as if he had no care in the world. In that bed, she saw a young boy, still innocent of the world's evil, who had dreams of being a writer, who would run in fields of grass just because he could. A young boy who loved the warmth of the sun on his face and the warm wind on his cheeks; a young boy not yet destroyed by the evil he could neither see coming nor understand its rationale.

They tried not to wake him up as they walked in, but the rustling of their feet opened his eyes. He looked at his mother and immediately gave a weak smile. In a still hoarse voice, he said, "Hey, Mom."

Mrs. Bryant immediately burst into tears.

"Hey, baby. How are you?" almost running to his

bedside and hugging and kissing her son.

"I am OK. I'm tired, so very tired."

"Oh, my Bobby, rest now. Rest," and with those words she caressed his head and gave him another kiss on his forehead.

"Hey, Bobby," said Sarah.

Looking in her direction, he replied, "Hey, Sis. How are you?"

"Who cares about me? I am so happy you are doing better."

"Yeah," said Dr. Bob.

"This is my husband, Bobby. Jonathan Meyers."

"Hello, Jonathan," said Dr. Bob. His fatigue was evident, and as they spoke his words became more difficult to utter.

"Wow! Someone was actually crazy enough to marry you?" said Dr. Bob with a weak smile.

Sarah nudged him saying, "Shut up!"

It was amazing: the dark cloud of his addiction lifted almost immediately after his father's death. It should not have happened according to the medical textbooks. His withdrawal from the opiates he was abusing should be in full swing now: he should be agitated, and sweaty, and hyper, and shaky. But, he was the calmest he has been in years. No one on the medical team understood it. What's more, since his hand was so shaky, when he pulled the trigger to try and kill himself, he only grazed his head. He had no significant injury.

"OK, honey, we'll get going to give you some rest," said Mrs. Bryant.

"Don't go!" he said weakly. "I must tell you this now." He paused for a moment and took a deep breath in.

"You must know by now that I was abusing intravenous drugs."

There was silence. Somehow, that fact did not reach Sarah and Mrs. Bryant. Dr. Bryant took their silence as his cue to continue.

"I was despondent. I lost all hope of a normal, happy life. I hated being who I was: a surgeon, a doctor, a son of a father who was so evil to so many people, a son whose own mistakes were covered up by that same father, a negligent brother, and a terrible son."

The silence continued.

"I was going to end it all, let go of this horrific existence. But, I came back, and I was enraged. Earlier, I tried to kill my father."

Everyone in the room gasped in shock.

"I disconnected him from the ventilator. But, when the alarms started going off, I chickened out and could not see my plan through. So, I wanted to kill myself. By the way, how is Dad?"

Mrs. Bryant started to cry, and she couldn't control her tears and sobs. She turned away from Dr. Bob's bed. It is unclear if her tears were from the reminder that her husband is dead, or that her son tried to hasten that end, or from the anger of Dr. Sanders' actions.

Sarah stepped up to her brother and held his hand.

"Dad died yesterday. That Dr. Sanders refused to continue the Code and he died shortly thereafter," said Sarah who was also crying. Jonathan was rubbing her shoulder as she spoke.

Dr. Bob, upon hearing the news, simply looked out into the dazzling view of the afternoon sky behind the shining city that was in clear view from his room window. After a long pause, he continued.

"Mother, I am going to pay for my crime."

This startled Mrs. Bryant and she turned quickly to his bedside.

"What did you say?"

"I am going to pay for my crime, mother."

"What are you talking about? I don't care what you

did. You need to be home with me, where I can take care of you, nurse you to health, make you well again. I have been robbed of that for too long."

"Mother, the police have already been here. I am already under arrest," and with that he lifted up his handcuffed hand, which no one had noticed was there.

"My God!" gasped Mrs. Bryant.

"There is no point in escaping. I have been escaping everything about my life for far too long. This is the destiny I have chosen for myself. Let me finally take the path that I have chosen for myself."

"Bobby..."

"Mother, my decision is final!" said Dr. Bob in an unusually strong manner, which caused him to go into a coughing spell.

Mrs. Bryant backed down, as she did not want to rile her son up any further. She had no intention of seeing her son go to jail, but she did not reveal this to him at this moment. She figured he will simply forget about it, and she will try to pull some strings with the police. After all, Dr. Bryant Jr. was the most prominent physician in all of Chicago. *Surely*, she thought to herself, *this must count for something*. She will talk to the detectives tomorrow, in fact. But, she let this go for now, looking at her watch.

"Oh my! It is almost time for your father's memorial

service. We had better get going. It would be very improper if Dr. Bryant's own family did not show up at his memorial service! Get some rest, my dear. We will see you tomorrow," and with that she bent down and kissed her son.

"See you later," he said. He then turned his head and closed his eyes. Almost instantaneously, he fell asleep.

Sarah swooped down and kissed her brother as well, and whispered in his ear, "Love ya, big bro." With those words, he woke up and grabbed her hand.

"Sis," he whispered, and Sarah leaned down with her ear to his mouth.

"You were never dead to me. At first, I was so angry at you. So angry that you left because…because I wanted to go with you…" Dr. Bob started to cry. "But I was too much of a coward."

Sarah started to cry as well.

"But, I swear…I swear…I anguished over you every single day you were gone. When I saw you, I was overjoyed with ecstasy. I just could not show it. You were never, ever dead to me."

Sarah kissed him once more on the forehead, unable to say anything.

"What's wrong, babe," Jonathan whispered to his wife as they were walking out of the room.

"Nothing," said Sarah, wiping her tears.

The Conference Room in which the memorial service was held was not very far from the ICU. The room was very nicely set up: rows and rows of chairs were neatly arranged. There were two tables to the side with drinks and snacks and cups laid out for people to enjoy. The podium was set up, and behind it was a large screen with a large photo of the late Dr. Bryant. It is amazing to realize how much pain, sorrow, and suffering could be behind such a large, confident, and beaming smile. There were two people, a man and a woman, who were playing a violin and harp to the side of the large screen. They were instructed to begin playing at around 4:30 PM.

"Oh my God!" said Mrs. Bryant. "They really went all out for this memorial service."

"Wow!" exclaimed Sarah.

"I wonder why no one has shown up yet," said Jonathan.

"They are all busy, and it's not yet five," said Mrs. Bryant. "Rest assured, they will come."

"Well," said Jonathan, "there's no harm in starting to eat before everyone else. It is, by the way, my father in law being honored here."

Sarah rolled her eyes. At the same time, however, she liked the fact that he said that. Jonathan's hatred for her father was no secret, but somehow, it softened when he came to Chicago.

Five o'clock came, and still, no one showed up. The service was supposed to end at 6PM. They all waited until 6:30 PM. No one showed up, not even the chaplain who made the announcement over the hospital loud speaker. Stunned, they all slowly walked out of the Conference Room and walked toward the elevator. They all left the hospital without saying a word and went home for the night.

As they were walking out, the man and woman playing the very soothing music continued out of courtesy, and when they were safely out of hearing distance, they both stopped, packed up their things, and left. The man playing the violin grabbed a Diet Coke on his way out.

25

"Prominent, Dedicated Chief of Surgery, Loving Father Touched the Lives of Many"

That was the title of the prominently displayed obituary in the largest daily newspaper in Chicago. Jonathan, as he was sipping his coffee, read the obituary to his mother-in-law, who was sitting across him on the large, ornate table in their enormous, gourmet kitchen. She sat silently listening to the obituary she composed for the public. It was a glowing summary of Dr. Bryant's long and successful life:

One of the city's most prominent cardiovascular surgeons, L. William Bryant, M.D., was chief of Cardiovascular Surgery at Chicago Memorial Hospital. He tragically lost his life Monday May 15 from metastatic cancer and overwhelming infection. "His death was an absolute shock. He was so healthy, so full of life. I can't believe he is gone," said Anne Bryant, his wife of 25 years.

Born into a middle-class working family, Dr. William Bryant worked hard his entire life to better himself and his family. The first of his five brothers and sisters to go to college, Dr. Bryant graduated at the top of his class at Thompson High School before attending the University of Chicago. He graduated summa cum laude with a degree in Biochemistry and attended the University of Chicago Medical School. He did his residency training at Northwestern University and then moved to Chicago Memorial Hospital, where he stayed for his entire medical career.

At Chicago Memorial, he quickly showed why he was the best of the best: improving on surgical techniques and recruiting the best cardiovascular surgeons in the country to his program. Under his tutelage, Chicago Memorial Hospital's cardiovascular surgery program became one of the top five in the country. He inspired so many to greatness including his son, Robert Bryant, who followed in his footsteps.

Yet, not only was Dr. Bryant accomplished in the medical field, but he also excelled in the area of philanthropy. Donating millions of dollars to a number of Chicago area charities, Dr. Bryant always had the poor and less fortunate on his mind. "I have been blessed so much," Dr. Bryant used to say, "that there is no way I could not give back to the community that gave me so much."

"Dad was such an inspiration for me. He made me the best doctor I could be," said the younger Dr. Bryant. He was becoming a prominent surgeon in his own right, and he has vowed to uphold the excellence his father instilled in everyone and everything at Chicago Memorial Hospital. "My father will always be a guiding force for me," said his daughter Sarah.

"He will be sorely, sorely missed."

Just before he died, he was awarded the Alfred J. Harrison Chair of Surgery for the Hospital. He is survived by his loving wife Mary, his grieving son Robert, his beloved daughter Sarah, and her husband Jonathan. Visitation will be held from 3pm to 7pm this Friday at Murray Funeral Home on State Street, with funeral service to follow. The family requests donations to the American Cancer Society in lieu of flowers and cards.

"That's perfect," said Mrs. Bryant. "Did they print his picture I sent?"

"Yes."

The picture was prominently displayed in the left upper hand corner of the obituary. The obituary took the entire half page. Everyone who knew anything about Dr. Bryant the father scoffed at the obituary, including Dr. Frank. He even posted it in the Doctor's Lounge, and it received innumerable laughs and chuckles. Someone even wrote "Asshole" next to his picture. It was not crossed out.

"Have you seen Sarah?" asked Mrs. Bryant.

"She's still sleeping. I haven't seen her sleep this much..."

They were interrupted by a large crash and thud, with things breaking. They were both startled and immediately ran upstairs to see what was the matter. Jonathan made it there first and found Sarah destroying her old bedroom, sobbing all the while.

She pulled down the bookshelf, throwing everything on the floor, and pulling off the pictures and posters on the wall. Her mother kept her room exactly the same ever since Sarah ran away from home all those years ago.

Sarah could not go into the room when she first came back to the home in which she endured so much pain. But, somehow, she mustered enough courage to walk into her old bedroom, and all the horrific, terrible memories came crashing back with a vengeance. All of the sounds, all of the smells, all of the feelings came back with an intensity that seems real. It was too much for her to bear.

When she turned and saw Jonathan, with her mother not that far behind, she fell to the floor and screamed and sobbed in tremendous anguish. Jonathan rushed to try to break her fall, but he did not make it. He then caressed his wife on the floor and tried to soothe her anguish. Suddenly, Mrs. Bryant went to Jonathan and tapped him on the shoulder.

"Jonathan, let me talk to her," she said.

He looked up at his mother-in-law, and he saw a determination that he heretofore had never seen, although tears were streaming down her face as well. Mrs. Bryant kneeled down on the floor and took Sarah from her husband's arms. She then held her daughter tight into her arms and Sarah buried her face into her mother's shoulders, screaming into her blouse. It rapidly became wet with Sarah's tears. Mrs. Bryant rocked her daughter and kept saying,

"It's OK, my precious Sarah. It's OK. He is gone now. He will never hurt you again."

It was something she should have done years ago, and she was trying, somehow, to make up for all those years of neglect. They sat in that embrace for a very long time, and neither of them wanted it to end. For the first time, Sarah felt comforted and protected by her mother, and that feeling was so soothing to her. Jonathan, for his part, stood over them crying like a baby himself.

26

The room was extravagantly furnished, with the most ornate floral arrangements money could buy. There were candles everywhere, and the soft sigh of violin and harp music played in the background, the same musicians who played for Dr. Bryant at the hospital. Several rows of chairs were arranged neatly facing the front of the room, where the casket was placed. At each side of the casket were pictures of Dr. Bryant with Mrs. Bryant, friends, and co-workers. None of the smiles were genuine except for Dr. Bryant's. As you entered the room, to your immediate right was an open guest book where visitors can sign and give good wishes.

The casket was the most ornate and fancy at the funeral home. He had on his most expensive suit he owned, yet in death, he seemed to be in anguish. Most people look rested and in peace after death, especially if they have suffered the pain of chronic illness. Not so Dr. Bryant. His face, though subtle, showed clear pain and anguish. Mrs. Bryant noticed this and complained to the funeral director, but no matter what he did, he could not erase the look of pain. Mrs. Bryant spent many an hour trying to come up with the perfect story to explain away to funeral-goers that look of pain on his face.

That effort, however, was in vain. The wake was between 3PM and 7PM, and notices were placed everywhere across the city and the hospital. That is in addition to the huge obituary in the paper. Surely, people knew when and where Dr. Bryant's wake was going to be held. Yet, no one came. The only ones at the wake were Sarah, Jonathan, Mrs. Bryant, and George. Bobby was still in rehab in the hospital and could not come.

For four agonizing hours, they waited for anyone to show up. No one. In the room next to theirs was another wake for a cab driver who also passed away the day before. His name was Aftab Muhammed, an immigrant from Bangladesh. All throughout the afternoon, scores of people streamed past the "Bryant room" with mourners, friends, and co-workers, coming to pay their final respects to Mr. Muhammed. Some were crying, some were laughing, some were expressionless. With each lull, Mrs. Bryant hoped against hope that someone, one person, would come and pay his or her final respects to her husband.

No one came.

Except for Ashraf: he was a co-worker of Mr. Aftab Muhammed. As he walked out with the others, he could not help but notice the empty Bryant room. He was on his way to bury his long-time friend, as is Islamic custom to bury the deceased as soon as humanly possible. Tears were in his eyes from saying goodbye to his good friend, as he walked into their room. Everyone stood for him, thinking he was someone Dr. Bryant knew. He walked up to them.

"I am very sorry for your loss, miss," said Ashraf in a thick, Bangladeshi accent.

"Thank you very much Mr...." said Mrs. Bryant.

"Ahmed. Ashraf Ahmed, ma'am."

"Did you know my husband?"

"No, ma'am. I just came as a fellow human being, to pay my respects to him. Our Prophet Muhammad, peace be upon him, taught us to respect the dead. So, I am here to do just that, ma'am."

They were all speechless. Ashraf did not want to stay long, and he felt a bit uncomfortable at their stunned silence.

"Well, good day to you ma'am. I am very sorry once again." Then, he turned and left.

They remained speechless as he walked out of the room, and Mrs. Bryant began to silently cry, full of anguish that no one came to pay their respects to her husband. Sarah could not bear to see her mother's anguish and left the room in tears as well.

"Sarah? Sarah!" said Jonathan running after her outside.

They both left Mrs. Bryant alone with George, and she sat on a very ornate chair and continued to cry, with her head bowed down in one hand. George came to comfort her.

"It's OK, ma'am," said George, filled with pity and remorse. He knew of many of the things his employer used to do. He drove Dr. Bryant Jr. and his many, many mistresses all around town. He was too much of a coward to say anything to Mrs. Bryant. Partly because he did not want to lose his job, which paid very, very well, and partly because he did not want to crush Mrs. Bryant's nicely equipped lifestyle. *What she does not know won't hurt her*, he used to always say to himself. Little did George know that Mrs. Bryant knew what was happening the entire time.

"Sarah! Stop, please, honey," said Jonathan running after his wife who was walking briskly down the sidewalk. The sun was setting, and the orange sunlight and shadows were everywhere. He caught up to her and put his hand on her shoulder.

"I just can't believe it! No one? No one came to Dad's wake?"

"Honey, your father hurt a lot of people. A LOT of people."

She turned around with a look of sharp anger.

"Hey! That's my father you're talking about!"

Jonathan could not believe it.

"Well, it's true."

"Have some respect! The man is dead!"

"I guess the pain he caused lives on."

"What is wrong with people today? I came back to face him, to let him know that I forgave him. How could it be that people could not have any compassion to pay respects to someone as prominent as my father? At least out of respect for his living and grieving family?"

"What's more important, baby, is that his family is by his side. That is most important, in fact. C'mon, let's go back inside and be with your Mom. The wake is about the end."

They both walked back inside

Mrs. Bryant went one last time to her husband's pained face and kissed him on the forehead, her eyes full of tears. She could not conceal her pain. Sarah and Jonathan both saw her mother quietly crying by the casket of her late husband, and Sarah walked up behind her, grabbed her by the shoulders, and said gently,

"C'mon Mom, let's go home. We have a long day

ahead of us tomorrow."

Mrs. Bryant put her hand over Sarah's, which was on her mother's shoulder, and they all walked out of the funeral home. George was waiting for them outside, and they all climbed into the car and went home. After they left, the funeral home worker went into the room where Dr. Bryant's casket was. He looked at his face and was surprised to see the pain on it. He then closed the casket and left the room, turning out the light behind him.

27

Sarah couldn't sleep that night. Her sleep was never sound anyway, but coming back home only made it worse. Jonathan being by her side did help, despite his sometimes loud snoring. Tonight, however, no sleep came to her eyes, despite her enormous fatigue. The house was quiet, and the sounds of her footsteps on the Brazilian cherry floors were the only sound she heard...until she walked downstairs toward the kitchen.

At the foot of the winding, curved staircase in the middle of the large, ornate curved foyer of the house, she saw the orange glow of a fire burning in the fireplace in the living room to her left. To her right was an equally ornate dining room, fully furnished for a dinner party that will never occur. Sarah turned to walk toward the glow and saw her mother, sitting in a chair, facing the fire. The orange light of the flames cast an eerie glow on her face, and she sat motionless staring into the fire, which danced and swayed with the wind drafts coming from the chimney.

"Mom?"

She didn't turn to Sarah.

"Mom? You alright?" Sarah asked as she walked closer to her mother.

"I simply can't believe it."

"What's wrong, Mom?"

"I simply can't believe it. All lies."

"Mom? What are you talking about?"

"All the times I saw people smiling in our faces: they were all lies. Our whole life...was one big lie. Now that he is gone, I don't understand how we lived that life for so long."

She turned and looked up at Sarah, who looked at her mother with concern.

"And the worst part...is that I let it destroy you and Bobby. I will never forgive myself for that."

She closed her eyes as tears began to stream down her face. Sarah reached out and held her mother's shoulder.

"The thing is, once you lie enough times to everyone else, you begin to believe it yourself. I let myself believe that everything was alright."

"Mom?" asked Sarah. Her mother opened her eyes and looked at her daughter again.

"Why didn't you leave? Why did you stay with him all those years, despite everything he did to you...to...to all of us?"

Mrs. Bryant began to cry more forcefully, but still quietly. She didn't answer for what seemed to be a very long while.

"I...I loved him. That was my curse...He always came home to me, and that was enough for me to stay and avoid doing what I knew *in my heart* was the right thing to do...Oh Sarah! I'm so, so sorry..." She buried her face into Sarah's stomach.

"Oh Mother!" said Sarah, holding on to her mother tightly.

"Everything will be ok. We will get through this together. We will make this new reality a beautiful one. Perhaps, with Dad's death, we can all be reborn anew. Perhaps, with Dad's death, we will be whole again, we will be made right."

Mrs. Bryant looked up at Sarah and managed to smile through her tears. They both sat together and watched the dancing flames until the morning, not saying a word to each other.

Jonathan came downstairs and saw his wife and

mother-in-law sitting by the fire, the glow of which was less prominent as the rays of the rising sun were beginning to enter into the room.

"You guys were sitting here all night?"

They were both slightly startled and looked back to find a still somewhat sleepy and disheveled Jonathan yawning and looking at them with surprise.

"We couldn't sleep," said Sarah.

"Well, today's a big day for all of us, with the funeral and all. You guys are gonna be tired."

"That's nothing a good cup of coffee won't cure," said Mrs. Bryant. "Come on, I will make a fresh pot." She then got up and went to the kitchen, and Jonathan put his hand on Sarah's shoulder.

"Everything alright, baby?"

"Yeah."

Jonathan then hugged his wife.

"Soon, this will all be over, and we will go back home to Seattle where we belong. We will put this painful episode of your life behind you, and you can live your life again."

"Yeah." Sarah was so comforted by his hug. "I'm so happy you are here, baby."

"I couldn't be without you, my love."

As they embraced, the smell of the fresh pot of coffee percolated into the room.

"Mmmm. There are few things I savor more than a freshly brewed cup of coffee," said Jonathan, now eager to get to the kitchen.

"I can't believe you would leave me for a cup of coffee!" said Sarah, only half joking.

"Sarah," whined Jonathan. "I'm hungry!"

"I will remember that the next time you want to make love," said Sarah.

"Baby, you know I love you more than anything in the world. You know that, without you, I would cease to exist as the person who I am. You know that..."

"Ok, Ok, I know. I was just kidding," smiled Sarah. They both walked into the kitchen, and Jonathan had his coffee, and they all ate breakfast. They then got ready for the funeral, getting dressed in the best clothes they had to lay their Dr. Bryant to his final resting place.

***

"OK, Dr. Bryant. You are all set for discharge. Do you have any questions?" asked Sarah, his nurse on the floor.

"No, thank you," said Dr. Bob quietly. He got up out of the room and walked straight to the police officer waiting for him at the nurses' station. The officer put handcuffs on him, and he escorted him outside of the hospital. There was an investigative reporter waiting outside for them, and he started asking Dr. Bob several questions. They ignored him, and the officers placed Dr. Bob into the car and drove off. In the car, Dr. Bob knocked on the partition between him and the two officers in the front. They opened it up and asked him what he needed.

"Can you take me somewhere, please?"

"We can't do that, sir."

"Please, sir. Please. My father is being buried today. I just want to say goodbye. I know I pointed a gun at him, and I have to pay for my crime. But, please, please, just let me say goodbye to him. Please, sir."

The look on Dr. Bob's face was pitiful, and it moved him to talk about it to his partner. They agreed to take him to the cemetery.

***

Sarah, Jonathan, Mrs. Bryant, and George went to the funeral home, expecting a large number of cars to be waiting to be a part of the funeral procession. Not one car was there. They only car they saw was the hearse carrying the casket. The funeral director had prepared a large number of stickers saying "Funeral" on them to be placed on the cars so that they can drive through red lights. He didn't need them, and this shocked him.

"Man," he said to the hearse driver, "he must of really pissed people off." The driver nodded in agreement, and then turned to the approaching Bryant car. After it stopped, Mrs. Bryant came out of the car and met the hearse driver, a chubby man of 55 named Thomas Scaliata.

"Mrs. Bryant?" Thomas said.

"Yes."

"I'm Thomas Scaliata, the driver of the hearse. We are all ready to go, ma'am."

"Is there no one for the funeral?" said Mrs. Bryant in shock.

"No one has shown up so far, ma'am. And we've been out here for at least 2 hours. Should we wait longer?"

"No...no. Let's go," said Mrs. Bryant dejectedly. By now, it should not have surprised her that no one was here, but it still shocked her nonetheless.

She got back into the car and they followed to hearse to the cemetery. The plot was already dug and ready for the casket. As the two cars parked in front of the lot, everyone was shocked that no one was there waiting.

"All lies...all lies," said Mrs. Bryant.

"Mother, it's OK. We are here. That is most important," said Sarah, holding her mother's hand. They all got out, and Jonathan, George, and Thomas all went to move the casket to the gravesite. They struggled to keep it from falling to the ground. It is supposed to be carried by six people, but there were no other people around to help them.

After the casket was placed on the machine that will lower the casket in the ground, Mrs. Bryant looked around in total amazement. Father O'Malley promised her he would be there for the funeral, but he didn't show up yet.

"He promised me he would be here," she said in amazement. "He couldn't have alienated *every single* person in Chicago? He was our pastor for over 30 years! He baptized the both of you! What is going on here?"

Actually, Dr. Bryant did alienate every single person with whom he came into contact. Dr. Bryant knew about certain allegations made against Fr. O'Malley, which were completely false and unsubstantiated. Yet, he threatened to leak them to the press and the Archdiocese of Chicago if Fr. O'Malley had ever told anyone about his abuse of his children. With the hysteria around abusive priests abound, Fr. O'Malley dared not cross Dr. Bryant. Yet, he resented him for it for the rest of his life. It is as Mrs. Bryant said: Fr.

O'Malley's smiles were all lies.

After a long wait, Sarah spoke up.

"Today, we lay to rest Dr. L. William Bryant. Father, husband, prominent physician, and community leader. His life was picture perfect: successful surgeon and distinguished professor; loving husband and father; dedicated philanthropist. Yet, underneath that veneer of beauty was a deep pain. No one could see it, no one knew about it, but it was there. And it was real..."

Sarah began to cry.

"And you hurt so many people, Dad. You hurt me in ways unimaginable and unbecoming of a truly loving father. You hurt Bobby in equally unspeakable ways. You hurt Mother by your repeated betrayals and infidelity. You hurt your co-workers and acquaintances to the point that no one - not a single person - with whom you have come into contact bothered to show up and pay their final respects. I never thought someone's ill will could reach such a proportion that, in death, the truth of all those smiles, and accolades, and honors would all be shown to be lies and feigned praise."

Sarah paused for a moment, and Jonathan held his wife's hand in support. Sarah then continued:

"Yet, we are here. Despite everything you have done to us, we are here. We are paying our final respects to you, because, despite all the pain you caused, you are still my father, her husband, and his father-in-law."

She pointed to her family as she said those words. "*We* refuse to be like *you*. We will never be like you. But, we are here, Dad. And, now, I say again, that I forgive you. The scars of your evil will always be with me; they will always hurt, but I will move on. I will be better. I will be stronger. You will not win. And so I pray that the Lord bring you some sort of peace and rest in this grave. Did you ever realize what you did? Did you ever feel pain for what you caused? Did you ever have an ounce of regret? We will never know. Still, I ask the Lord to have mercy on your soul. Because I am not like you..."

Sarah could no longer speak from her crying. Jonathan hugged his wife and tried to comfort her as much as possible, tears streaming down his face.

Sarah then turned around and decided to wait in the car, with Jonathan joining her there. She sat in the car crying, and Jonathan sat silently next to her, holding her hand and kissing it over and over.

Mrs. Bryant, tears in her eyes, walked up to the casket and could only find these words:

"I will always love you. And for that, I am truly sorry."

And she kissed her two fingers and pressed them to his casket. She also turned to the car and got in. George, with his hat off, turned to the casket and said quietly,

"Rest in peace, Dr. Bryant."

He then turned and went to the car, and they all drove off. The casket stood there, alone and firm in the howling wind. Not too long after they left, a police car pulled up to the grave site. Out came Dr. Bob, in handcuffs, escorted by the two police officers. They were both on edge, afraid he would try to pull something in the cemetery. He walked up to the casket and stood silently before it.

Suddenly, an uncontrollable rage came over him and he kicked the casket with all his might, hurting his toe is the process. The jolt, however, somehow caused the casket to fall into the grave with a violent crash. The door opened up and the face and upper torso was revealed, showing his face in pain. Dr. Bob looked into the grave, saw his father's face, and spit into the grave.

"I hope you burn in Hell...you rotten piece of shit!"

He then spit again in his grave, and told the officers, in shock at what just transpired, "I am done, here." They both led him, silent and limping, to the police car and put him in and they drove away. They arrived in the police station, booked him, and put him in a holding cell until he awaited arraignment the following morning.

"Do you want to make a phone call, or anything doctor?" asked the officer.

"No," he said stoically.

They left him in his cell, and he lay on the slab of granite called a "bed" and closed his eyes. He quickly fell asleep.

28

"Doctor?"

Dr. Bob woke up from his deep sleep.

"There is someone here to see you."

Mrs. Bryant had retained an attorney for her son, but he did not want to talk to him until after he was discharged. Yet, Dr. Bob did not want to tell his mother when that day was. He wanted to be convicted and go to jail as quickly as possible, and he knew his mother would retain the best criminal defense lawyer money could buy for him. He did not want the hassle of trials, hearings, and the like.

The person sent to see her son was his attorney, James Fitzgerald, the most prominent criminal defense attorney in Chicago. He was managing partner of Fitzgerald, Thomas, and Duke. Unbeknownst to Dr. Bob, a staff member called Mrs.

Bryant the day after discharge to check up on him, since he wasn't answering his own phone. She immediately called Mr. Fitzgerald.

"You get my son out of jail right now!" she screamed on the phone.

"Dr. Bryant?" said James.

"Yes?"

"I am your attorney, James Fitzgerald."

Dr. Bob rolled his eyes and turned his back to him.

"Sir, your mother retained me as Counsel."

"I have no need for your services. I have already confessed my crime to the police. I am going to pay for what I have done."

"You need to stop saying things like that, sir. It will harm your defense..."

Dr. Bob shot up in fury.

"I don't need a defense! I am in charge here! I do not need your services. Good day, sir."

"Dr. Bryant..."

"GOOD DAY SIR!"

"Clearly, you are not thinking straight. I will come

back a different time. Thank you for your time."

"My thinking is quite clear! I am not in need of your services, dammit! Don't come back!"

He got up and screamed those words into his face through the jail cell bars. Mr. Fitzgerald was taken aback, and he turned and walked away, opening up his cell phone and making a phone call to Mrs. Bryant.

"Officer! Officer!"

An officer came to his cell: "Yes, doctor?"

"I do not want to be disturbed by anyone. I do not care who it is. No one is to see me. I want to be left alone."

"Sure thing, doc."

He has already made a signed confession at the hospital, so there was no need for Mr. Fitzgerald to try to stay any longer and talk to his reluctant client. One thing he did notice, however, was how well written his statement was. Billy had always wanted to be a writer, but his father would hear nothing of it. He even secretly wrote stories and hid them from his father. When he found them, he burned them all in the fireplace.

When Mrs. Bryant heard what had happened from Mr. Fitzgerald, she rushed to the police station herself to try to talk some sense to her son.

"I'm sorry ma'am. He has specifically requested that he sees no one."

"What do you mean? I am his mother! You have no right to bar me from seeing him."

"Ma'am, I am very sorry, but Dr. Bryant specifically told us that he does not want to see anyone."

"He is not well. I demand you take me to see him at once!"

"There is nothing I can do ma'am."

"This is an outrage! The chief of police will hear about this!"

"His number is 312-254-3425." Several officers around him chuckled.

"You haven't heard the last of me!" said Mrs. Bryant storming out of the police station. She was deeply offended by his sarcasm.

"Crazy bitch," said the officer under his breath as she walked out.

Later that morning, Dr. Bob was arraigned. He tried to go through the hearing without his Counsel, but he came just before the hearing started, and told the judge:

"Your Honor, I am James Fitzgerald, counsel for Dr.

Bryant."

"I have no need for Counsel, your Honor," said Dr. Bryant.

"I understand, but I think it is in your best interest, doctor," said the Judge.

The courtroom was packed, and Sarah, Jonathan, and Mrs. Bryant were sitting just behind the table at which her son and his attorney sat.

The bailiff read out loud the case against Dr. Bob, with various charges being made against him.

The judge asked Mr. Fitzgerald: "How does the defendant plead?"

"Uh...the defendant pleads..."

"Mr. Fitzgerald! SIT DOWN!" screamed Dr. Bob.

"Dr. Bryant, I am your counsel..."

"SIT DOWN!" he screamed even louder.

The courtroom spectators murmured to themselves over this unbelievable spectacle. Mrs. Bryant, with tears in her eyes, was unable to remain silent.

"Bobby! What is the matter with you?"

The judge clapped his gavel.

"I will have order in this court."

Without looking at his mother, he said to the judge: "Your Honor, I would like to address the Court and make my plea. I do not want Counsel's services."

"It is in your best interest..."

"I understand, your Honor," Dr. Bob interrupted. "Please, let me address the Court."

"Proceed, doctor."

"Your honor. My father was a brutal, evil man. He abused me both physically and sexually for years on end. I thought it was something that fathers do to their sons. It stopped, however, when my sister was born. The things he did to her were unspeakable, and he led her to run away from our home at the age of 15..."

Sarah could not control herself and began to cry. All eyes turned to her. Dr. Bob continued, but before doing so, he reached back and squeezed her hand.

"He repeatedly betrayed my mother, the one who stood by him despite all the terrible things he did to all of us. He was successful, yes, but he betrayed everyone he came into contact with. He does not know how to not hurt people. All of the smiles given to him were fake. Yes, he was honored. Yes, he was a prominent force in Chicago. But, he got there by destroying anyone who came in his way. He destroyed me. I have never wanted to be a physician. I wanted to be a writer. But, my father forced me into this field, and I have hated my existence ever since. All my life, I did not have the courage to stand up to him. I tried to defend my sister from him, but he brutalized me time and again, that I simply gave up.

I will never..." Dr. Bob choked up with tears, "never forgive myself for that.

"To try to ease the miserable pain of my existence, I abused drugs, and they nearly killed me. When I realized that my life had become nothing but ruin, I was devastated. That devastation turned to pure and unmitigated rage; so, I bought a gun and tried to kill myself. But before I turned the gun on myself, I pointed it at my mother and my father. So many times, your Honor, I wish I didn't miss my head." And he pointed to the scar on the side of his head from the gun shot.

This made Mrs. Bryant break down. The courtroom was in stunned silence.

"My father was an evil, brutal man. Yet, he was still my father. I should not have done what I did. And therefore, I must pay for my crime. I plead guilty, your Honor."

The courtroom suddenly was abuzz with gasps and talking.

The judge hit his gavel once more and yelled: "Order!"

"Doctor, do you understand what you are doing? Do you understand what this means?"

"Fully, your Honor."

"Well, we will have sentencing in one month. Take Dr. Bryant into custody."

"Thank you, your Honor."

Mrs. Bryant could not believe her ears, and James Fitzgerald was shocked beyond words.

The officers came to handcuff Dr. Bob and take him back to jail.

As he was going out of the courtroom, Mrs. Bryant stopped her son.

"Bobby, what are you doing? How could you give up your own freedom? You are not a criminal!"

"Mother, I have never been more free in my entire life than I am right now. I love you, now and forever."

He turned to his sister:

"I'm sorry I wasn't there for you, sis. I love you so much."

Sarah could not take it and wept.

"Don't go, Bobby!" she said. She grabbed his hand,

but it came loose as he was led away from her.

They all watched him be led out of the courtroom and back to the jail cell where he will await sentencing.

At around the same time, two messengers were dispatched from the same building that the hearing was held to two different locations in the city. Each messenger carried an identical package for two different people. The first messenger arrived at an apartment not far from the courthouse. He knocked at the door, and Dr. Sanders opened the door.

"Dr. Sanders?"

"Yes."

"A summons for you."

"What?"

"Have a good day, sir."

The messenger turned and walked away. Dr. Sanders closed the door and walked back to the couch, frantically opening the manila envelope. His heart sank when he read the first page: It was a court document, a summons for him to appear because of a lawsuit. He was a defendant in a wrongful death lawsuit filed against the hospital by the estate of L. William Bryant, M.D. As he read the complaint, he became despondent and angry.

"Son of a bitch!" he exclaimed, slamming down the large packet on the coffee table in front of him.

Soon after Dr. Sanders got his summons, the other package arrived at the office of Dr. Frank at Chicago Memorial Hospital. He knew immediately what it was and cursed when the envelope was given to him by his secretary. He opened up the envelope and took one look at it:

"Son of a bitch!" he screamed and threw the package on the floor. His hands were trembling in rage.

29

The fog was still thick and heavy over the ground. The dew was dripping off of the tall, thick grass at the base of the forest, and the orange sunlight was just peeking over the horizon, making the thick fog shine more brightly white than before. About 50 miles away from this forest, next to which Dr. L. William Bryant was buried, Mrs. Bryant, Sarah, and her two children: Bobby 4, and Annie 2, were in a car waiting for Dr. Bob to walk out of his apartment building. Five years have passed, and he was finally leaving Chicago after years of persistence on the part of his mother.

His courtroom speech to the judge so moved both him and the prosecution, that they downgraded his charges and he was out of jail several months later. He has since left the practice of medicine, and has started his writing career in earnest.

Mrs. Bryant sold her home, and the estate's extensive

possessions fetched several tens of millions of dollars, with which she supported both Sarah and Dr. Bob. She moved to Seattle to be with her daughter, and they lived a very, very comfortable lifestyle. Sarah's children (and their children) will be taken care of for decades to come. The lawsuit against the hospital and Dr. Sanders is still ongoing, and Mrs. Bryant flies to and from Chicago whenever she is needed for a deposition or other hearing.

As Dr. Bob walked out, tasting the crisp May morning air, his smile was ear to ear. He rushed to embrace his mother, who was too choked up with tears to say anything at all. They hugged for a very long time. Sarah waited eagerly to hug her brother, and their embrace was equally long.

"Who is this handsome young lad?" asked Dr. Bob, who aged quite considerably over the five years. Yet, with that age came poise and distinction.

"I'm Bobby, and I'm four," said his nephew. He looked at Sarah and was deeply moved, but he could not say a word.

"It's nice to meet you, Bobby."

"And this," said Sarah, "is your niece Annie."

"She's beautiful."

They were both blue-eyed and blonde haired. Their faces glowed with an innocence that seemed to overwhelm anyone who saw them. It was as if they carried with them the innocence of their mother and uncle that was lost to them many years ago. They both imbued a beauty that was truly indescribable.

"Let's go. Our flight is in four hours."

"Wait! I must go to the cemetery first."

"What! That's fifty miles from here! We will never make it to O'Hare on time!"

"Mother, this is something I must do. I will miss my flight if it comes to that."

"There is unresolved business that I must take care of."

"We better make it on time," said Mrs. Bryant.

"We will, mother, we will."

"C'mon babies. Let's get back into the car," said Sarah.

"Let's go, George. Step on it to the cemetery. We have a flight to catch," said Mrs. Bryant.

"Yes, ma'am," said George. After the house was sold, Mrs. Bryant gave George a hefty amount of money as final compensation. He used the proceeds to start his own limousine business. He was doing very well, and whenever Mrs. Bryant was in town, he would personally drive her wherever and whenever she wanted free of charge.

Amazingly, the car ride to the cemetery was faster than normal, and during the ride, Mrs. Bryant protested once more, "Why are were going to the cemetery, again?"

Dr. Bob's face became serious and he began to speak, looking out of the window at the passing traffic:

"Soon after I got to prison, I was awakened by someone tapping my foot. I opened my eyes to see Dad standing in front of me."

"Oh my God!' exclaimed Mrs. Bryant.

"I nearly fell out of bed and staggered back to the wall of the cell. 'What are you doing here?' I asked. 'You're dead.' 'I am very much alive, son,' he said, and with those words he fell to his knees and came to my feet. 'I am suffering, son, a torment unspeakable.' 'Death approaches me from every corner, yet I am not dead. I cannot rest. I cannot breathe. I cannot see. I am enveloped in the evil which I have wrought with my own hands. So, I come to you, son, to beg your forgiveness.'"

They were all silent.

"Dad continued, 'Son, I am sorry for all that I have done. I am sorry for the evil I brought upon you, the evil I did to your sister, the betrayal of your mother. I am sorry for all the human relations I broke to achieve a fleeting worldly success. I did have sorrow for what I did in this world, but I was too cowardly to admit it, too arrogant to acknowledge it and change my errant ways. Please, forgive me. Please, tell your sister, I am sorry. Please, tell your mother, I am sorry."

Tears began to stream down the faces of Sarah and her mother.

"I didn't tell you about this until now, because, it took me a very long time to come to terms with what Dad had done. As he pleaded with me, his head at my feet, I stood there and didn't say a word to him. I was both terrified and hurt and angry at the same time. I wanted to kick his head, but I was paralyzed by my fear and anger. I looked away from him and then, suddenly, when I looked back he was gone. I don't know if I was dreaming or hallucinating. But, that incident always stayed with me. It has never happened since."

"Here's the cemetery," said George, equally in awe at the story. He turned into the cemetery and drove to section 33, the place where both his father and grandfather are buried. The car stopped in front of the section where the gravesite was. They erected a large marble tombstone which read, "L. William Bryant, M.D. Born 1950, Died 2012. Dedicated Physician, Loving Husband, Committed Father."

As they watched Dr. Bryant walk up to his father's grave, thoughts emerged of that day five years ago when they stood, all alone, paying their final respects. As he walked up to his father's grave, he remembered his fit of rage and his spitting on his father's grave, much in the same way - although unbeknownst to him - his father spat on his grandfather's grave.

He looked at the tombstone, paused for a moment, with the wind blowing his graying hair gently, and reached into this long coat pocket and pulled out a rose. He laid the rose at the foot of the tombstone and uttered silently,

"Rest in peace, Dad."

He then turned away, got into the car, and drove off to the airport.

ABOUT THE AUTHOR

Hesham A. Hassaballa is a Chicago doctor and writer. He has written extensively on a freelance basis, being published in newspapers across the country and around the world. He has been a Beliefnet columnist since 2001, and has written for the Religion News Service. He is also a columnist for Patheos.

His articles have been distributed worldwide by Agence Global, and he was also a guest blogger for *The Chicago Tribune* before joining ChicagoNow. In addition, Dr. Hassaballa has appeared as a guest on WTTW (Channel 11) in Chicago, CNN, Fox News, BBC, and National Public Radio.

Dr. Hassaballa is co-author of *The Beliefnet Guide to Islam* (Doubleday), and his essay, "Why I Love the Ten Commandments," was published in the award-winning book *Taking Back Islam* (Rodale). His previous book, *Noble Brother*, is the story of the Prophet Muhammad told entirely in poetry.

In addition to writing, Dr. Hassaballa serves on the board of directors of the Chicago chapter of the Council on Islamic Relations. He also co-founded the Bayan Hassaballa Foundation and currently serves as its Executive Director. He lives in the greater Chicago area with his wife and four children.

Made in the USA
Las Vegas, NV
01 April 2023

70007569R00146